The Author an

Kevin Crossley-Holland, poet, storyteller, anthologist, librettist and broadcaster, lives in North Norfolk and has a deep love and knowledge of East Anglia and the Fens. His many books include *Poems from East Anglia*, *The Penguin Book of Norse Myths*, the Carnegie Medal-winning *Storm*, a translation of *Beowulf* and a collection of very short stories called *Short!* His classic collection of *British Folk Tales* is shortly to be reissued by Orion as *Folk Tales of Britain and Ireland*, with illustrations by Emma Chichester Clark.

The King Who Was and Will Be: the World of King Arthur and his Court, was published by Orion to rave reviews in 1998. It is the start of a whole series of books on King Arthur by Kevin Crossley-Holland.

John Lawrence's work can be seen in the V & A, the Ashmolean Museum and collections in the USA. His drawings and engravings appear in over a hundred books for children and adults, including *Watership Down* by Richard Adams (Penguin), *A New Treasury of Poetry* compiled by Neil Philip (Blackie) and currently *The Mysteries of Zigomar*. He studied engraving under Gertrude Hermes in evening classes at the Central School of Art and is regarded as one of this country's leading engravers. He and his wife live in Cambridge.

BY THE SAME AUTHOR

The King Who Was and Will Be
Tales from the Old World

The Old Stories

Folk Tales from East Anglia and the Fen Country

Kevin Crossley-Holland

With illustrations by
John Lawrence

Dolphin Paperbacks

5 0 1 1

First published by Colt Books in 1997
This edition published as a Dolphin paperback in 1999
by Orion Children's Books
a division of the Orion Publishing Group Ltd
Orion House
5 Upper Saint Martin's Lane
London WC2H 9EA

Earlier versions of the stories in this book first appeared in
The Dead Moon and *Long Tom and the Dead Hand*,
published by André Deutsch in 1982 and 1992,
and in *British Folk Tales*, published by Orchard Books in 1987.

A catalogue record for this book is available from the British Library

Typeset at The Spartan Press Ltd, Lymington, Hants

Printed in Great Britain by The Guernsey Press Co. Ltd, Guernsey, C. I.

ISBN 1 85881 753 6

for Rosemary Crossley-Holland
with love

CONTENTS

FOREWORD

No matter where a folk tale comes from, its subject is always the same. It's you! And me! We *are* the story

A folk tale is a kind of rapid word-illustration. 'Just look at human beings!' it says. 'This is what they're really like. This is the amazing mixture each one of them is made of – kind one moment, unkind the next; brave but nervous; they're windbags; they've got hearts of gold; they laugh, they cry; they're eager for friends but need to be alone; they look forward, they look back. . .' Recognise yourself?

In one of The Old Stories, a daredevil boy takes one risk too many, and comes to a sticky end; in another, a girl who refuses to be scared off by ghosts or pretend-ghosts gets rich. Two lovers are forcibly separated by disapproving parents but united in death. An oaf is saved by his wife's brains. A dreamer wakes up and sets off after his dream . . . These tales come from one part of Britain, the east, and many were told for hundreds of years before they were written down, but they tell us a thousand things about ourselves – our own characters, our hopes and fears and wild imaginings.

Between the tales, like little pieces of a jigsaw, are short pieces of prose and verse found in medieval letters and chronicles, folk beliefs, extracts from modern diaries and books about East Anglia. Why? Because each of them somehow relates to the tale that follows it, and each earths that tale either in the landscape, society or situation from which that tale springs. At the end of the book, I have given the sources for these pieces and for the old stories themselves.

TH ATSAL L!LO OKE AST!

Kevin Crossley-Holland
Burnham Market, May 1999

'I reckon it's best . . .
to sort of believe nothing
and everything, in a way.'

AN OLD MAN IN LINCOLSHIRE

Yallery Brown

✢

It was a Sunday night in July and Tom was in no hurry to get back to High Farm. He didn't like hard work and nothing but hard work awaited him – another week of grooming the horses, mucking out the stables, doing odd jobs at all hours around the farm.

So Tom took the long way round from his parents' home. He wandered along the path that led across the west field and down to the dark spinney some people said was haunted. Tom was happy to be out in the moonlight, out in the wide and silent fields and the smell of growing things. It was warm and still and the air was full of little sounds, as though the trees and grass were whispering to themselves.

Then, all at once, Tom heard a kind of sobbing somewhere ahead of him in the darkness. He stopped and listened and

thought it was the saddest sound he had ever heard – like a little child scared and exhausted and almost heartbroken. The sob-sobbing lapsed into a moan and then it rose again into a long, whimpering wail.

Tom began to peer about in the darkness. He searched everywhere, but though he looked and looked, he could see nothing. The sound was so close, at his very ear, spent and sorrowful, that he called out over and again, 'Whisht, child, whisht! I'll take you back to your mother if you'll only hush now.'

Tom searched under the hedge that ran along the edge of the spinney. Then he scrambled over it and searched along the other side. He searched among the trees in the spinney itself. Then he waded through the long grass and weeds, but he only frightened some sleeping birds, and stung his hands on a bunch of nettles.

Tom stopped and scratched his head, and felt like giving up. But then, in the quietness, the whimpering became louder and stronger, and Tom thought he could hear words of some sort. He strained his ears and, mixed up with the sobbing, he made out the words, 'Oh! Oh! The great big stone! Ooh! Ooh! The stone on top!'

Tom started to search again. In the dark, he peered here and peered there and at last, down by the far end of the hedge, almost buried in the earth and hidden amongst matted grass and weeds, he found a great flat stone.

'A Strangers' Table,' said Tom to himself, and he felt uneasy at the thought of meddling with it. He didn't want to cross the little people and bring ill luck on his head by disturbing their moonlight dancing-floor. All the same, he did get down on his knees and put an ear to the stone.

At once he heard it clearer than ever, a weary little voice sobbing, 'Ooh! Ooh! The stone, the stone on top!'

Uneasy as he was about touching the thing, Tom couldn't

bear the sound of the little child trapped under it. He tore like mad at the stone until he felt it begin to shift and lift from the earth. Then, with a sigh, the great slab suddenly came away, out of the damp soil and tangled grass and growing things. And there, in the hollow, was a little creature lying on his back, blinking up at the moon and at Tom.

He was no bigger than a year-old baby but he had long tangled hair and a long beard wound round and round his body so that Tom couldn't even see his clothes. His hair, like a baby's hair, was all yellow and shining and silken; but one look at his face and you would have thought he had lived for hundreds and hundreds of years – it was just a heap of wrinkles, with two shining black eyes, surrounded by masses of shining yellow hair. The creature's skin was the colour of freshly-turned earth in the spring, as brown as brown could be; and his hands and feet were just as brown as his face.

He had stopped moaning now but the tears still shone on his cheeks. He looked quite dazed by the moonlight and the night air.

While Tom wondered what to do, the creature suddenly scrambled out of the hollow and stood up and began to look around him. He didn't reach up to Tom's knee and Tom thought he was the strangest thing he had ever set eyes on: brown and yellow all over, yellow and brown, with such a glint in his eyes, and such a wizened face, that Tom felt afraid of him for all that he was so little and so old.

In a while, the creature got used to the moonlight. Then he looked up and boldly stared Tom in the eye. 'Tom,' he said, as cool as you like, 'you're a good lad.' His voice was soft and high and piping like a bird and he said it a second time. 'Tom, you're a good lad.'

Tom pulled at his cap and wondered what to reply. But he was so scared that his jaw seemed locked; he couldn't open his mouth.

'Houts!' said the creature. 'You needn't be afraid of me. You've done me a better turn than you know, my lad, and I'll do the same for you.'

Tom was still too scared to reply but he thought to himself, 'Lord, he's a bogle, and no mistake!'

'No,' said the creature, quick as quick. 'I'm not a bogle, and you'd do better not to ask me what I am. Anyway, I'm a good friend of yours.'

Tom's knees knocked together when the creature said that. He knew no ordinary being could read thoughts. But still, the creature seemed so friendly and reasonable that, in a quavery voice, he managed to say, 'May I be asking your honour's name?'

'H'm,' said the creature, and he pulled his beard. 'As for that . . .' and he thought for a moment. 'As for that, yes, Yallery Brown you can call me. Yallery Brown. That's what I am, and it'll do as well as any other name. Yallery Brown, Tom; Yallery Brown is your friend, my lad.'

'Thank you, master,' said Tom meekly.

'And now,' said the creature, 'I'm in a hurry tonight, but tell me quickly, what shall I do for you? Do you want a wife? I can give you as much gold as you can carry. Or do you want help with your work? Only say the word.'

Tom scratched his head. 'Well,' he said, 'as for a wife, I've no wish to get married; wives spell nothing but trouble, and I've got a mother and sister to mend my clothes. and as for gold, that's as maybe . . .' Tom grinned and thought that the creature was boasting and couldn't do as much as he had offered. 'But work,' said Tom. 'There! I can't stand work and if you'll give me a helping hand I'll thank . . .'

'Stop!' said the creature, quick as lighting. 'I'll help you and you're welcome. But if ever you say that word to me – if ever you *thank* me – you'll never see me again. Beware! I want no thanks and I'll have no thanks, do you hear me?' Yallery

Brown stamped one little foot on the ground and looked as wicked as a raging bull.

'Mind that, now, you great lump!' said Yallery Brown, calming down a bit. 'And if ever you need help, or get into trouble, just call for me and say, "Yallery Brown, come from the earth, Yallery Brown, I want you." Just call for me and I'll be at your side at once. And now,' said Yallery Brown, picking a dandelion puff, 'goodnight to you.' And he blew the dandelion seed into Tom's eyes and ears. When Tom could see again, the little creature had disappeared; and but for the uprooted stone and hollow at his feet, Tom would have thought he had been dreaming.

Then Tom went back home instead of going up to High Farm, and he went to bed; and in the morning he had almost forgotten about Yallery Brown. But when he did go up to work at the farm there was nothing to do! It was all done already: the horses were groomed, the stables were mucked out, everything was neat and tidy, and Tom had nothing to do but sit around with his hands in his pockets.

It was just the same the next day, and the day after. All Tom's work was done by Yallery Brown, and done better than Tom could have done it himself. And if the farmer gave Tom more work, Tom simply sat down and watched the work get done by itself. The singeing irons, the besom and this, that and the other all set to and got through their tasks in no time. For Tom never saw Yallery Brown out in the light of day; it was only in the darkness that he saw him hopping about, like a will-o'-the-wyke without his lantern.

To begin with, Tom couldn't have been happier. He had nothing to do, and got well paid for it! But after a time, things began to go wrong. Not only was Tom's work done but the work of the other farmhands was undone: if his buckets were filled, theirs were upset; if his tools were sharpened, theirs were blunted and wrecked; if his horses were clean as daisies, theirs were splashed with muck. That's how things were, day in and day out, always the same.

The other farmhands saw Yallery Brown flitting around night after night; they saw things that worked without helping hands; and they saw that Tom's work was done for him, and their work was undone for them. Naturally they began to fight shy of Tom. After a while, they wouldn't speak to him or even go near him. And, in the end, they all went to the farmer and told him what was happening.

Tom often thought he would be better off doing his own work after all, and he wished Yallery Brown would leave him and his old friends in peace. But he couldn't do a thing about it – brooms wouldn't so much as stay in his hand, the plough ran away from him, the hoe kept slipping out of his grip. He could only sit on his own, while all the other lads gave him the cold shoulder and Yallery Brown worked for him and worked against all the others.

At last, things got so bad that the farmer gave Tom the sack; and if he hadn't, all the other farmhands would probably have sacked the farmer, for they vowed they would no longer stay on the same farm with Tom.

Tom was angry and upset then. It was a very good farm, and he was well paid; he was hopping mad with Yallery Brown for getting him into such trouble. And, without thinking, he shook his fist and shouted as loud as he could, 'Yallery Brown, come out of the earth; Yallery Brown, you scamp, I want you.'

Tom had done no more than close his mouth when he felt something tweaking the back of his leg. It pinched him and he jumped, and when he looked down, Tom could scarcely believe his eyes – for there already was the little creature with his shining hair and wrinkled face and wickedly glinting black eyes.

Tom was in a fine old rage and he would have liked nothing

so much as to give Yallery Brown a big kick, but the creature was so small he would only have slid off the side of his boot. Tom scowled and said, 'Look here, master! I'll thank you to leave me alone from now on, do you hear me? I want none of your help, and I'll have nothing more to do with you. Understand?'

The horrid little creature gave a screech of a laugh and pointed a brown finger at Tom. 'Ho, ho, Tom!' he said. 'You've just thanked me, my lad, and I told you not to, I told you not to!'

'I don't want any of your help, I tell you,' yelled Tom. 'I only want never to see you again, and to have nothing more to do with you.'

The more Tom said, the more Yallery Brown laughed and screeched and mocked. 'Tom, my lad,' he said with a devilish grin, 'I'll tell you something, Tom. It's true enough I'll never help you again, and call on me as you will, you'll never see me again after today.'

'Good,' said Tom.

'But I never said I'd leave you alone, Tom, and I never will, my lad! I was nice and safe under that stone, Tom, and I could do no harm. But you let me out yourself, and you can't put me back again.'

Tom grimaced and shook his head.

'I would have been your friend,' said Yallery Brown, 'and worked for you if you had been wise; but since you're a born fool, I'll give you nothing but fool's luck. When everything goes wrong and arsy-versy, you'll know it's Yallery Brown's doing, even if you can't see him. Mark my words, Tom!'

And Yallery Brown began to dance round Tom, looking like a little child with all his yellow hair, but looking older than ever with his grinning, wrinkled face. And as he danced, he sang:

Work as you will
You'll never do well;
Work as you may,
You'll never make hay;
For harm and bad luck and Yallery Brown
You've let out yourself from under the stone.

The words rang in Tom's ears over and again. Then Yallery Brown just looked up, grinning at Tom and chuckling as wickedly as the devil himself.

Tom was terrified. He could only stand there, shaking all over, staring down at the horrible little creature.

Then Yallery Brown's shining yellow hair lifted and rippled in a gust of wind. It wound round and round him so that he looked for all the world like a great dandelion puff. And then the little creature floated away on the breeze over the wall and out of sight; as he went, Tom could hear the last skirl of an insult and a sneering laugh.

Tom was scared to death and, after that day, his fortunes took a tumble. He worked here and worked there, he put his hand to this and that, but something always went wrong.

The years passed by and Tom married and had children. But his children died and his wife didn't – when she scolded him, people could hear her a mile off, and Tom did think now and then he could have done without *her*! And although he tried his hand with cattle and sheep and pigs and goats and hens, none of them fattened as they should. Nothing ever worked for him.

No, Tom had no luck at all after meeting Yallery Brown. For the rest of his life, until he was dead and buried and maybe afterwards, there was no end to Yallery Brown's spite towards him. And day after day as long as he lived, even as an old man when he sat trembling beside the fire, Tom heard a voice singing:

Work as you will
You'll never do well;
Work as you may,
You'll never make hay;
For harm and bad luck and Yallery Brown
You've let out yourself from under the stone.

As you came from the holy-land
  Of Walsingham,
Met you not with my true love
  By the way as you came?

How should I know your true love,
  That have met many a one
As I came from the holy-land,
  That have come, that have gone?

She is neither white nor brown,
  But as the heavens fair;
There is none hath a form so divine
  On the earth, in the air.

Such a one did I meet (good sir)
   With angel-like face;
Who like a queen did appear
   In her gait, in her grace.

ANONYMOUS

The Pedlar
of Swaffham

✢

One night John Chapman had a dream. A man stood by him, dressed in a surcoat as red as blood; and the man said, 'Go to London Bridge. Go and be quick. Go, good will come of it.'

John the pedlar woke with a start. 'Cateryne,' he whispered, 'Cateryne, wake up! I've had a dream.'

Cateryne, his wife, groaned and tossed and turned. 'What?' she said.

'I've had a dream.'

'Go to sleep, John,' she said; and she fell asleep again.

John lay and wondered at his dream; and while he lay wondering he too fell asleep. But the man in scarlet came a

second time, and said, 'Go to London Bridge. Go and be quick. Go, good will come of it.'

The pedlar sat up in the dark. 'Caateryne!' he growled. 'Wake up! Wake up! I've had the same dream again.'

Cateryne groaned and tossed and turned. 'What?' she said. Then John told her his dream.

'You,' she said, 'you would believe anything.'

The moment he woke next morning, the pedlar of Swaffham remembered his dream. He told it to his children, Margaret and Hue and Dominic. He told it to his wife again.

'Forget it!' said Cateryne.

So John went about his business as usual and, as usual, his mastiff went with him. He fed his pig and hens in the back yard. He hoisted his pack on his broad shoulders and went to the marketplace; he set up his stall of pots and pans, household goods of one kind and another, phials and potions, special trimmings for ladies' gowns. He gossiped with his friends – the butcher, the baker, the smith, the shoemaker and the weaver, the dyer and many another. But no matter what he did, the pedlar could not escape his dream. He shook his lion-head, he rubbed his blue eyes, but the dream seemed real and everything else seemed dreamlike. 'What am I to do?' he said.

And his mastiff opened his jaws, and yawned. That evening John Chapman walked across the marketplace to the tumbledown church. And there he found the thin priest, Master Fuller; his holy cheekbones shone in the half-light. 'Well, what is it?' Master Fuller said. Then John told him about his strange dream.

'I dream, you dream, everyone dreams,' said the priest impatiently, swatting dust from his black gown. 'Dream of how we can get gold to rebuild our church! This ramshackle place is an insult to God.'

The two of them stood and stared sadly about them: all the

walls of stone were rickety and uneven; the roof of the north aisle had fallen in, and through it they could see the crooked spire.

John Chapman gave a long sigh. 'Gold,' he said. 'I wish I could.'

Then the pedlar left the church and went back to his small cottage. But he was still uneasy. Nothing he did, and nothing anyone had said, seemed to make any difference; he could not forget his dream.

That night Cateryne said, 'You've talked and talked of the man with the surcoat as red as blood. You've been more dreaming than awake. Perhaps, after all, you must go to London Bridge.'

'I'll go,' said John. 'I'll go and be quick.'

Next day, John Chapman got up at first light. At once he began to make ready for his journey. He hurried about, he banged his head against a beam, his face turned red. 'I must take five gold pieces,' he said. 'I must take my cudgel.'

'You must take your hood,' said Cateryne.

Then John looked at his mastiff. 'I must take you,' he said. And the mastiff thumped the ground with his tail; dust and chaff flew through the air.

'Tell no one where I've gone,' said John Chapman. 'I don't want to be the laughing-stock of Swaffham.'

Then, while the pedlar ate his fill of meat and curds, Cateryne put more food into his pack – cheese, and two loaves made of beans and bran, and a gourd full of ale.

So everything was ready. And just as the June sun rose behind a light cloud, a great coin of gold, John kissed his wife and his children goodbye.

'Come back!' called little Dominic.

They stood by the door, the four of them, waving and waving until the pedlar with his pack, his cudgel and his mastiff, had walked out of Swaffham; out of sight.

John Chapman strode past the archery butts just outside the town; he hurried between fields white with sheep. At first he knew the way well, but then the rough highway that men called the Gold Road left the open fields behind and passed through sandy heathland where there were no people, no sheep, no villages.

Soon the rain came, heavy, blurring everything. John pulled his hood over his head, but the water seeped through it. It soaked through his clothes and dripped from his nose.

By midday, he was tired and steaming. So he stopped to eat food and give a bone to his mastiff. And while they ate, some lord's messenger, decked out in red and blue, galloped by and spattered them with mud.

'The devil take him!' the pedlar said.

During the afternoon, the rain eased and the pedlar and his dog were able to quicken their pace. One by one, the mile-stones dropped away; they made good progress.

But that evening it grew dark before the pedlar could find any shelter, even a peasant's shack or some deserted hovel. John had no choice but to sleep in the open, under an oak tree. 'God help us,' he said, 'if there are wolves.'

But there were no wolves, only strange nightsounds: the tree groaning and creaking, wind in the moaning leaves and wind in the rustling grass, the barking of fox and vixen. When first light came, John could barely get to his feet for the ache in his cold bones and the cramp in his empty stomach.

And his mastiff hobbled about as if he were a hundred.

So for four days they walked. Each hour contained its own surprise; John talked to a friendly priest who had been to Jerusalem; he kept company with a couple of vagabonds who wanted him to go to a fair at Waltham; he shook off a rascally pardoner who tried to sell him a ticket to heaven; he saw rabbits, and hares, and deer; he gazed down from hill-crests at tapestries of fields; he followed the way through dark forests where only silence lived. Never in his life had John seen so many strangers nor set eyes on so many strange things. 'I'll tell you what,' he said to his mastiff, 'you and I are foreigners in our own country.'

Sometimes the pedlar's pack chafed at his shoulders; often he envied the many travellers with horses – pilgrims and merchants, scholars and monks; but not for one moment did he forget his purpose. For as long as it was light, John Chapman made haste, following the Gold Road south towards London. And each night, after the first, he stayed at a wayside inn.

On the morning of the fifth day, the pedlar and his dog came at last to the City of London. At the sight of the high walls, John's heart quickened, and so did his step.

And his mastiff leaped about, barking for excitement.

They hurried through the great gate; and there before them were crowds of people coming and going, to-ing and fro-ing; men shouting their wares; women jostling and gossiping; small children begging; and many, many others sitting in rags in the filthy street. And there were houses to left and right; and after that, more houses, more streets, and always more people. John had never seen such a sight nor smelt such a stink nor heard such a hubbub.

A tide of people swept him along until he came to a place where four ways met. There, John stopped a man and asked him the way to London Bridge.

'Straight on,' said the man. 'Straight as an arrow's flight, all the way.'

The broad river gleamed under the sun, silver and green, ruckled by wind; gulls swooped and climbed again, shrieking. The great bridge spanned the water, the long bridge with its houses overhanging the river. It was a sight to gladden any man. And when he saw it, John Chapman got to his knees.

He thanked God that his journey had been safe, and that he had come at last to London Bridge.

But the moment the pedlar stepped on to the bridge itself he felt strangely foolish. All his hope and excitement seemed long ago. People were passing this way and that, but no one so much as looked at him. No one took the least notice of him. Having at last found London Bridge, the poor pedlar of Swaffham felt utterly lost.

He walked up and down; he stared about him; he watched boats shoot the bridge; he added up his money. Hour after hour after hour went by; the pedlar waited.

Late that afternoon, a group of pilgrims on horseback gathered on the Bridge. And they began to sing: *As you came from the holy-land of Walsingham* . . .

'Walsingham!' cried John. 'I know it well. I've taken my wares there a hundred times. Will this song explain my dream?'

As if to answer him, the group of pilgrims broke up and rode off, still singing, even as he hurried towards them.

'Wait!' bawled John. 'Wait!'

But the hooves of the horses clattered and the poor pedlar was left, in the fading light, looking after them. John felt heavy-hearted. He wearily asked a passer-by where he might stay, and was directed to The Three Cranes, a hostelry on the riverbank, a stopping-place for passengers coming down the river, a sleeping-place for travellers in all weathers.

There John Chapman and his mastiff shared a bed of straw; they were both dog-tired.

Early on the morning of the second day the pedlar and his dog returned to the bridge. Once again, hour after hour went by. But late that day John saw a man with matted red hair lead a loping black bear across the bridge. 'Look!' he exclaimed delightedly.

And his mastiff looked, carefully.

'A rare sight!' said John. 'A sight worth travelling miles to see. Perhaps here I shall find the meaning of my dream.' So the pedlar greeted the man; and he thought he had never seen anyone so ugly in all his life. 'Does the bear dance?' he asked.

'He does,' said the man. He squinted at John. 'Give me gold and I'll show you.'

'Another time,' said the pedlar. And he stepped forward to pat the bear's gleaming fur.

'Hands off!' snapped the man.

'Why?' asked John.

'He'll have your hand off, that's why.'

The pedlar stepped back hastily and called his mastiff to heel.

'He had a hand off at Cambridge,' said the man.

'Not the best companion,' said John.

'He'll bite your head off!' growled the man, and he squinted more fiercely than ever.

So the second day turned out no better than the first. And on the third day the poor pedlar waited and waited, he walked up and down and he walked to and fro, and no good came of it. 'Now we have only one piece of gold left,' he said to his mastiff. 'Tomorrow we'll have to go home; I'm a great fool to have come at all.'

At that moment a man shaped like an egg waddled up to John. 'For three days,' he said, 'you've been loitering on this bridge.'

'How do you know?' asked John, surprised.

'From my shop I've seen you come and go, come and go from dawn to dusk. What are you up to? Who are you waiting for?'

'That's exactly what I was asking myself,' said the pedlar sadly. 'To tell you the truth, I've walked to London Bridge because I dreamed that good would come of it.'

'Lord preserve me!' exclaimed the shopkeeper. 'What a waste of time!'

John Chapman shrugged his shoulders and sighed; he didn't know what to say.

'Only fools follow dreams,' said the shopkeeper. 'Why, last night I had a dream myself. I dreamed a pot of gold lay buried by a hawthorn tree in a garden; and the garden belonged to some pedlar, in a place called Swaffham.'

'A pot of gold?' said John. 'A pedlar?'

'You see?' said the egg-shaped man. 'Nonsense!'

'Yes,' said John.

'Dreams are just dreams,' said the shopkeeper with a wave of his pudgy hand. 'You're wasting your time. Take my advice and go back home.'

'I will!' said John Chapman.

✜

So it was that, in the evening of the twelfth day after his departure, John Chapman and his dog – spattered with mud, aching and blistered, weary but excited – returned home. They saw the leaning church spire; they passed the archery butts; they came at last to John's small cottage of wattle and daub.

Cateryne had never in her life been so glad to see her husband.

Margaret and Hue leaped about and their ashen hair danced on their heads.

'Come back!' cried little Dominic.

'So,' asked Cateryne, 'what of the dream, John?'

Then John told them in his own unhurried way. He told them of his journey; he told them of the long days on London Bridge; and, at last, he told them of the shopkeeper's words.

'A man follows one dream and returns with another,' said

Cateryne. 'How can it all be true?'

'I've asked myself that a thousand times,' the pedlar said, 'and there's only one way to find out.'

The gnarled hawthorn tree stood at the end of the yard; it had lived long, perhaps hundreds of years. And now its leaves seemed to whisper secrets.

The hens clucked in the dusk; and the pig lay still, one eye open, watching John.

'I'll start here,' said the pedlar quietly. Then he gripped his round-edged spade and began to dig, making a mound of the loose earth.

'Can I?' asked Margaret.

'Let me!' said Hue.

'Wait!' said John. And again he dug. The spade bit into the packed soil.

At once they heard it, the grind of metal against metal, muted by soil. The pedlar took one look at his family and began to dig as fast as he could. Earth flew through the air. 'Look!' he gasped. 'Look! Look!' He had partly uncovered a great metal pot.

John tossed away his spade. He bent down and tugged. He worked his fingers further under the pot and tugged again. Then suddenly the dark earth gave up its secret. John staggered backwards, grasping the pot and, as he fell, the lid flew off. The ground was carpeted with gold!

At first they were all utterly silent. Only the tree, the tree in the gloom went on whispering.

'Well! Gather it up,' said the pedlar, slapping earth and straw from his surcoat with his great hands. 'Take it inside.'

They picked up the gold coins and put them back into the pot. Then they carried the pot into their cottage, and placed it on the floor in front of the fire.

'Look! What's this?' said Hue, rubbing the lid of the pot. 'It's writing.'

John frowned and shook his head. 'It's words,' he said. 'I know, I'll hide the gold here and take the empty pot with the rest of my wares to the marketplace. Someone is sure to come along and read it for us.'

Next morning the pedlar was early in the marketplace, and before long Master Fuller came picking his way towards him through the higgledy-piggledy stalls – a dark figure amongst bright colours, a silent man in a sea of noise. 'John Chapman,' he exclaimed. 'Where have you been?'

'To and fro,' said the pedlar.

'And where were you last Sunday?' asked the priest. 'I missed you at mass.'

'Well, I . . .'

'Excuses! Always excuses!' said the priest sharply. 'Who shall be saved? Men are empty vessels.' And he rapped the great metal pot with his knuckles; it rang with a fine deep note. 'Now that's a fine vessel!' said Master Fuller.

'It is,' agreed John Chapman.

'There are words on it,' said the priest. He raised the lid and narrowed his eyes. 'It's in Latin. It says, *Under me* . . . yes . . . *Under me there lies another richer than I.*' The priest frowned. 'What does that mean?'

John Chapman scratched the back of his head.

'Where did you get it?'

'Out of a back yard,' said the pedlar, shrugging his broad shoulders.

'I must go,' said the priest suddenly. 'All this idle chatter. Men would do better to give time to God.' And with that, the priest walked off towards the rickety church.

At once, the pedlar packed up his wares and hurried home.

'This time you shall dig,' he told his children.

Then Hue grasped the spade and began to dig; the rounded edge sheared through the darkness. His face soon flushed; he began to pant.

'Now let Margaret have it,' the pedlar said.

Hue scowled, and handed the spade to his sister.

Margaret threw back her hair and stepped into the pit, and dug yet deeper. Deeper and deeper. Then, once again, metal grated against metal – the same unmistakable sound. Margaret shivered with excitement. 'You,' she said, and handed the spade back to her father.

Once more John dug as fast as he could; once more he tugged and tugged; and once more the reluctant earth yielded its secret – a second great pot, an enormous pot twice as large as the first. The pedlar could barely heave it out of the hole and on to the level ground. When he levered off the lid, they all saw that this pot too was heaped to the brim with glowing gold. 'It's like a dream,' said John, 'and because of a dream. But we're awake, and rich.'

Cateryne stared into the gaping, black hole. 'Who hid it there?' she said. 'And why?'

'Someone who lived here before us?' said the pedlar. 'Or travellers on the Gold Road? How shall we ever know? People always say the hawthorn tree is a magic tree.'

'What are we going to do with it?' asked Cateryne.

For a moment John did not reply. His blue eyes closed, his face wrinkled. 'I know,' he said at last. 'I know. A little we'll keep – enough to pay for our own small needs, enough to buy ourselves a strip of land. But all the rest, every coin, we must give to Master Fuller to build the new church.' Cateryne drew in her breath and smiled and clapped her hands. 'Amen!' she said.

'Amen!' chimed the children.

'In this way,' said John, 'everyone in Swaffham will share in the treasure.'

'Now,' said Cateryne, 'and in times to come.'

That afternoon, John Chapman found the priest skulking in the gloom of the tumbledown church. 'Master Fuller,' he said, 'I can give gold for the new church.'

'You?' said the priest. 'Gold?'

'Wait here,' said the pedlar. He hurried out of the church and back to his cottage. There, he counted one hundred pieces of gold for his own needs and the needs of his family, and hid them in the inner room, under the bed of straw.

Then the pedlar and his wife, and Margaret and Hue, followed by Dominic and their loyal mastiff, carried the two pots to Swaffham Church. As they crossed the marketplace, they shouted to their friends, 'Come with us! Come to the church!'

So the butcher, the baker, the smith, the shoemaker, and the weaver, the dyer and many another left their work. In no time, a great procession, curious and chattering, were filing into the silent church.

In the nave, John and Cateryne turned one pot upside down. Then Margaret and Hue emptied the other. A great mound of coins glowed mysteriously in the half-light.

The townspeople gasped and Master Fuller's eyes gleamed. 'Explain!' he said.

So John Chapman told them the whole story from beginning to end. And no storyteller, before or since, has ever had such an audience.

'There's enough gold here,' said Master Fuller, 'to rebuild the north aisle, and the steeple.' Then he raised his right hand. 'Let us pray,' he said, 'and after that . . . let us sing and dance the night away.'

'Sing in the churchyard? Dance in the churchyard?' everyone cried.

'Even until this old church falls down,' said Master Fuller. And for the first time that anyone could remember, he laughed. He threw back his head and laughed.

So, that same evening, a man with a bugle and a man with a humstrum and a man with cymbals and clappers played as if they meant to raise the roof off every house in Swaffham. The townsfolk sang and danced until midnight. And John the dreamer was tossed by the dancers into the air, higher and higher, towards the stars.

And his mastiff sat on his haunches, and laughed.

Right reverend and worshipful and my very well-beloved Valentine, I commend myself to you with all my heart, wishing to hear that all is well with you: I beseech Almighty God to keep you well according to his pleasure and your heart's desire. If you would like to know how I am, I am not well in body or heart, nor shall be until I hear from you.

> *For no creature knows what pain I endure*
> *On pain of death, I dare not reveal it.*

My lady my mother has put the matter very diligently to my father, but she can get no more than you know of, which God knows, I am very sorry about.

But if you love me, as I hope indeed that you do, you will not leave me because of it; if you did not have half the estates you have, I would not forsake you, even if I had to work as hard as any woman alive.

And if you command me to keep me true
    wherever I go
Indeed I will do all I can to love you, and
    nothing more.
And if my friends say I do wrong, they shall not
    stop me from doing it.
My heart bids me to love you for ever
    Truly, over anything on earth.
However angry they are, I hope it will be better
    in future.

No more for now, but the Holy Trinity have you in keeping. Please do not let any creature on earth see this note, but only you. And this letter was written at Topcroft with a very sad heart.

By your own M.B.

MARGERY BREWS TO JOHN PASTON

The Suffolk Miracle

⁕

There was once a rich farmer in Suffolk. When he stood in the middle of his land, he could see nothing he did not own – fields of swaying corn and silken barley, a copse of pale ash trees, his farm and its outbuildings, hayricks and horses and all his farm machinery.

But much as he cared about his crops, the farmer cared even more for his daughter, Rosamund. With her pools of dark eyes and oval white face and waterfall of jet-black hair, she was as beautiful as any girl in the county. As she grew up, she was her parents' delight in all she thought and said and did.

But then Frank, the ploughboy, fell in love with Rosamund. Rosamund's eye brightened and her cheek flushed and she walked about with an inner smile. It was as if she were bewitched by him.

The farmer did not see things in this way. He thought no good could come of a match between a rich farmer's daughter and a poor ploughboy, and said as much to Rosamund.

Rosamund took no notice. In the early evenings, when the day's work was done, she spirited herself out of the farmhouse and away into the cornfields and her lover's arms.

The farmer and his wife decided to put an end to this business once and for all. Despite her protests and tears, they sent Rosamund away to stay with her uncle – the farmer's brother – forty miles away.

'There you'll go . . .' said her father.

'No,' cried Rosamund.

'. . . and there you'll remain until you've forgotten about this Frank.'

Frank could plough a straight furrow across a field; he could plough a whole field fair and square. But he was not a talker, he let the things he did speak for him.

When he was cut off from his Rosamund, Frank said even less. He left the farmer's service and took to walking all day by himself. He walked for mile after mile across the shining fields and along the green lanes of Suffolk. And if he talked at all, he talked to the birds and wild animals, talked to the wind.

Frank grew wan and thin; he took less and less pleasure in the breathing world around him; he lived in a dream and his dream was of Rosamund.

It was as if Frank were cut off from the spring from which his own life flowed. He lay in his bed. Did he even listen to what the doctor prescribed? Did he even hear what his family and friends said? It was no good. Frank the ploughboy was sick of love; he was incurable, and he died.

'Better not tell her,' said the farmer to his wife. 'Let her get over Frank in her own good time.'

✣

Although she was cut off from Frank, Rosamund did not give up hope. 'Love is stronger than time,' she said to herself, and thought that in time things might change: her parents would relent, or Frank would make his fortune, or something, or something.

One evening, about a month after Frank's death, Rosamund and her uncle were sitting in front of the fire when there was a tap on the door.

'Very late,' said her uncle, frowning.

Rosamund got up and drew back the bolt and opened the door.

'"Frank!" she cried. 'Oh Frank!' And Rosamund threw herself into her lover's arms.

'Rosamund,' said Frank. 'You're to come home with me. That's what your parents say.'

'Praise be to God!' cried Rosamund. 'I knew they would, I knew they would. And I will come home with you.'

Rosamund's uncle got up from the fire and joined them.

'Uncle,' cried Rosamund, 'this is Frank and he's come for me and I'm to go home with him.'

'I hoped as much,' said her uncle, smiling.

'Look!' said Rosamund. 'My father's best horse! My mother's hood!'

'Yes, I hoped it would come to this,' said Rosamund's uncle. 'True lovers never can be parted.'

Rosamund kissed her uncle goodbye and mounted behind Frank. They galloped out of the courtyard, and the horse's hooves struck sparks from the paving-stones. Rosamund put her arms round her lover's waist and they rode into the darkness.

'My head aches,' said Frank.

Then Rosamund pulled out her white handkerchief and tied it round Frank's forehead. 'My!' she said. 'Your forehead's cold. Cold as clay. We'll have a fire when we get home.'

Within three hours, Rosamund and Frank had covered forty miles and were back at her father's farm. Rosamund dismounted and patted the horse's steaming flank.

'You go in,' said Frank. 'I'll put the horse into the stable.'

Rosamund tried the front door; it was locked. So she went round to the back, and tried the kitchen door, but that was locked too. Then she rapped sharply, surprised there were no lights burning upstairs or downstairs, and no one to welcome her. Rosamund shivered under the stars and rapped again more loudly. At last there was a scuffling and a scrabbling inside and a voice called out, 'Who's there?'

'Rosamund.'

'Who?' said the voice.

'It's me, Rosamund.'

'Wait!' said the voice.

Rosamund frowned, and for a while there was silence. The owner of the voice, a sleepy farmhand, went upstairs and woke the farmer; and the farmer came stumbling downstairs in his nightshirt and unbolted the door.

'Father!' cried Rosamund.

'How did you get here?' said the farmer, astonished.

'What do you mean?' faltered Rosamund.

'How did you get here?' repeated the farmer.

'Didn't you send for me,' said Rosamund, gaily, 'and with your own horse? Frank came and collected me just three hours ago.'

'Frank?' echoed her father.

'He's got so cold,' said Rosamund, 'as cold as clay. I had to tie my handkerchief round his forehead.'

'Where is he then?' said the farmer quietly.

'Still in the stable,' said Rosamund.

'You come in,' said her father, 'and get ready for bed. I'll make sure the horse is well littered.'

Rosamund stepped into the farmhouse; its warmth seeped

into her and made her feel utterly weary.

The farmer, meanwhile, hurried round to the stable in his nightshirt. He raised his candle and peered about. There was no one there, and not a sound. But then he saw that his best horse was splattered with mud and sweating all over.

Slowly he made his way back to the house and slowly he walked upstairs to his daughter's room.

'So much to say,' said Rosamund sleepily. 'So good to be home again.'

'In the morning,' said the farmer gently. 'It's late now. You'll see him in the morning.'

❖

The farmer did not sleep, not for one minute. He lay on his bed, and tossed, and got up and dressed at first light. Then he walked round his farm, wondering what to do. He went back to the house and up to Rosamund's room. He woke her just as the sun broke the eastern horizon and flooded her bedroom with its yellow light.

'Father,' sighed Rosamund. 'Thank you.'

The farmer sat down on the end of his daughter's bed. 'Rosamund,' he said, 'I must tell you now: Frank is dead.'

Rosamund sat up, her dark eyes wide and terrified.

'He died a month ago. Your mother and I, we thought it best not to tell you.'

'It isn't true,' cried Rosamund. 'You know it isn't true.'

'It is true,' said the farmer, 'and we'll have to prove it.'

When Rosamund was dressed, she and her father went down to the little cottage where Frank's old father lived.

'One month ago now,' the old man said sadly, and he looked at the ground.

'It isn't true what you say,' cried Rosamund wildly. 'Why are you trying to hide him from me?'

'After last night, she won't believe it,' said the farmer.

'True love never dies,' said Frank's father.

'Well, there's only one way to settle it,' said the farmer. 'And settle it we must, or your son will go on walking and my daughter will go mad.'

The three of them found the sexton in the graveyard. They told him what had happened during the night and the sexton agreed to dig up Frank's grave. He dug and dug until he was waist-deep in the ground. Then he unearthed Frank's coffin and, as Rosamund and the two men stared down, he brushed away the earth and prised open the lid.

There lay Frank, one month dead, his body already turning to mould.

Rosamund screamed.

There lay Frank, one month dead, and he had a white handkerchief tied round his forehead.

Rosamund toppled into the grave. She was lifted out and taken back to the farm, and nursed night and day, but she never recovered. No, before long the two lovers lay side by side, sleeping cold in the churchyard.

 THEM ILL ERSLEA VET-HEMI!
LLT HEW HER RYME NLOW
ERTH EIRS-AILTH; EMA! LTS
TER SLE AVET-HE KI? LN,
FORAD-ROPO; FTH EWHI.
TESW ANA-LE-

TRADITIONAL (RHYMING SIGN IN AN INN)

What a Donkey!

✣

There were three students at Cambridge who worked a little, and talked a lot, and never had any money.

'We haven't even got enough to buy supper,' said the first.

'Then let's think how to get some,' said the second. 'We're not asses!'

'Would you rather be poor and clever or rich and stupid?' said the third student (whose friends called him Ned).

So the three students went out walking the streets of Cambridge, looking for a way to lay their hands on some money.

In the street leading to the market, they saw a donkey, with a handsome broad black stripe across its shoulders and a bushy tuft at the end of its tail. It was tethered to the handle of a cottage door.

'All right!' said Ned, the third student. 'I've got an idea.'

At once he bent down, untied the donkey's girth and lifted off its two empty baskets.

'What are you doing?' said the first student.

'Quick!' said Ned. 'Take off his bridle! Yes! Put it on me! And now put the baskets on my back.'

'What for?' said the second student.

'Untie the halter,' said Ned.

'Why?' said the first student.

'Get that donkey away as fast as you can,' said Ned. 'Sell it in the market! I'll meet you there as soon as I can.'

'Right!' said the first student and 'Right!' said the second student. And they hurried away with the donkey as fast as they could.

Before long, the donkey's owner came out of his little cottage, where he had been smoking a quiet pipe and drinking a pint of beer. He wasn't a rich man or a clever one; he was a tinker.

'What the devil's this?' he shouted, when he saw Ned with the baskets on his back, and the donkey's bit between his teeth. 'What's going on?'

'Excuse me, sir,' said Ned. 'I'll try to explain.'

'Who are you?' said the tinker.

'Seven years ago,' said Ned, 'I had a terrible argument with my father. A terrible argument, and he turned me into a donkey.'

'A donkey,' said the tinker.

'And for seven years,' said Ned, 'I've been kicked and cursed, and I've carried loads. You were my only kind owner.'

'Dear God!' said the poor man.

'But now, at long last, the seven years are over. They're over today, and you must set me free.'

'Of course! Of course!' said the tinker untying the girth and lifting away the two empty baskets, and then taking off the reins and bit.

'Thank goodness for that!' said Ned, giving himself a shake.

'What's your name, then?' said the poor man.

'Duncan,' said the third student. 'Duncan. My friends call me Ned.' And with that, the student shook hands with the poor man, and thanked him, and ran off down the street towards the market. But when he was safely out of earshot, he just threw back his head and brayed with laughter.

Poor as he was, the tinker decided he would have to buy another donkey, so that he could travel his odds and ends from fair to fair. Only a few days later, he walked ten miles to a nearby fair, and made his way straight to the animal pens. There were several donkeys for sale and, much to his surprise, the tinker immediately recognised one of them: there was no mistaking that handsome broad black stripe across its shoulders and the bushy tuft at the end of its tail.

When the donkey saw the tinker, it recognised him too, and began to bray. How mournfully it brayed, as if it were begging its owner to buy it back!

But the tinker would have none of it. 'So you've quarrelled with your father again, have you?' he said. 'Dang me if I'll buy you for a second time.'

There is a place far out on the sands somewhere between High Sand Creek and
Stone Mell Creek that is called Blacknock.
It is a patch of mud covered with zos grass
and full of blue-shelled cockles known as
'Stewkey blues'. It is a famous place for
widgeon, but very dangerous to get on to
and off, if one is not too certain of the way
on a dark night. The women cockle
gatherers from Stiffkey (or Stewkey, as it is
sometimes called) who have double the
strength of a normal man, go right out there
between the tides and get a peck of these
cockles and carry them back to the village,
miles across the sand and saltings.
Sometime during the early nineteen
hundreds, one of these almost superhuman

women got caught by the tide on Blacknock. A fog came on suddenly and she could not find her way back. The whelk boats from Wells got caught in it out at sea and came in all along the coast. The crews said they could hear the woman screaming in the fog on Blacknock. She took hours to drown in the shallow, seething water, and the terrible screaming went on and on all night, and they could not find her in the fog.

Next day she was there, drowned on Blacknock. They say that on foggy nights, when the sea moves uneasily beneath its white blanket and the gulls forsake the outer sandbars, you can hear her screaming still.

ALAN SAVORY

Long Tom and
the Dead Hand

✥

Long Tom Pattison was a wild slip of a lad. He was always larking around. No one had a word to say against him, though: for all his tricks, he was a decent lad – just too full of fun, and too waggle-headed to stop and think things through, most of the time.

There were heaps of stories about the marsh surrounding the village where Tom lived, stories about boggarts and horrors and the like. People were scared of gruesome things and never went out at night on their own.

After an evening in the inn, the men all hung around, and all walked home together. And even then, they disliked the shadows and the dark corners, and fingered their safe-keeps

all the way home. Almost everyone had a sort of charm to keep the evil things away – bits of paper with verses out of the Bible, crinkled up in a nutshell; three straws and a four-leaved clover tied with the hair of a dead man; spells written by a wise woman; or maybe the clippings of a dead woman's nails. If you could get them, they were the best safe-keep of all.

Well, Long Tom was just about the only lad in the place without a safe-keep, and everyone said that one day he'd regret it. His mother was always begging and beseeching him to carry the charm she'd got from old Molly, the wise woman who lived next to the mill.

But Tom only laughed and refused to take it. At closing time in the inn, he mocked the men because they were afraid of the dark; and he pretended to see things in the black corners, to make them more scared than ever.

But one night the men rounded on Tom. 'That's all right your making fun of us,' they said. 'But if you met a bogle, or had to cross the marsh in the dark, you'd be no better than the rest of us.'

Maybe Tom had drunk more beer than he ought to have done. Anyhow, the silly lad got all fired up. 'I'm afraid of nothing,' he shouted, 'nothing you can see and nothing you can't see. I'll cross the marsh alone, by lantern-light, on the darkest night of the year.'

There was a noisy argument in the inn that evening, but at last they calmed down a bit, and it was agreed Long Tom would walk the path across the marsh, and round by the willow-snag, on the very next night. 'And if you decide against it,' said the men, 'you must stop getting at other people for being afraid of the dark.'

'By God!' said the stupid creature. 'I won't break my word, I can promise you that. What a pack of fools you are! Why should I come to harm in the marsh, when I have to cross it almost every day as part of my job?'

Long Tom sounded so bold and confident that some of the younger lads began to think maybe he was right after all, and the bogles weren't as black – as the saying goes – as they were painted. But the older men knew better than that. They shook their heads and hoped no harm would come of the lad's disbelieving ways.

Well, they all thought Tom would regret his words next day, when he'd thought about things a bit; but for all that, as soon as it got dark the men and lads met at the corner of the green lane, near the cottage where Tom lived with his mother.

When they got there, they could hear the old woman in the kitchen, sobbing and scolding Tom; and they began to wonder whether, after all, the lad really meant to cross the marsh alone. And after a while the door was flung open, and out came Tom laughing like mad, and pulling away from his old mother, who was trying to put something into his pocket, and sobbing fit to break her heart.

'No, mother,' Tom was saying, 'I tell you, I'll have none of your charms and bobberies. Stop snivelling, will you? I'll be back before long, safe and sound. Don't you be a fool like the rest of them, do you hear me?'

Then Long Tom snatched the lantern from the old woman, and, mocking and laughing at the lads, he ran off toward the marsh. At this, some of the men tried to stop Tom, and begged him not to go.

'If you won't take back your words,' said one man – it was Willie Kirby – 'I'll take back mine. You can mock us as much as you like, but stay here! Don't go down to the marsh! You don't know what might happen to you.'

But Tom only laughed and snapped his fingers in Willie's face. 'That for the boggart!' he cried. 'And that for you too!' And away he ran.

Then the old men waggled their heads, and they went

home hoping for the best, but feeling terribly uneasy. Some of the youngsters, though, were ashamed to look afraid, seeing as Tom gave nothing for the horrors, and maybe a dozen of them followed him down the path that led to the marsh. They weren't all that sure of themselves, and were scared enough when they felt the earth was squishy underfoot, and saw the glint of the lantern falling on the black water holes next to the path. But on they went – Tom perhaps thirty steps ahead, singing and whistling as bold as can be, and the lads behind, bunched close together but getting less afraid as they went further and further into the marsh without seeing anything of the bogles and horrors.

As they drew near the willow-snag, though, the wind came up the valley with a long, soughing moan – chill and damp it came, straight from the sea – wailing as if it carried inside it all the evil things that live in the darkness and the shadows. Out went Tom's lantern, and the soughing wind was so chill and scary that the lad stopped singing, and stood stock-still by the willow-snag.

The boys behind felt worse than Tom did: they dared not go back and dared not go forward, they could only stand trembling and praying and squeezing their safe-keeps in the darkness, waiting for something to happen.

And then, the things that Tom had disbelieved in, they came, they did – the horrors of the air, and the horrors of the waters, and the slimy, creeping things, and the crying, wailing things – until the night, that had been so quiet and still, was full of moving shadows and dim grinning faces with blazing eyes and wailing voices.

Closer and closer they came round Long Tom as he stood with his back against the snag, hands in his pockets, trying to keep his spirits up. The very darkness seemed alive with shapes, and the air was thick with their wailing.

By now, the lads behind Tom were down on their knee-bones, praying for dear life, and calling on the saints, and the Virgin Mary, and the wise women, to save them. They could see Tom was standing with his back against the stump, and saw his white face and furious eyes through the shadows thronging between them.

And after a while, so they said afterwards, they heard Tom shouting and swearing as the black things came closer and closer; they were only able to catch glimpses of him, and then Tom threw up his arms, and he appeared to be fighting and struggling with the things around him; and by-and-by they could hear nothing but the skirling and laughing and wailing and moaning of the horrors, and see nothing but the shifting blackness of the crowding shapes, until all at once the darkness opened out and right in front of them they saw Long Tom standing by the snag, with his face white as death and with staring eyes. He was holding on to the willow with one hand, and the other was stretched out and gripped by a Hand without a body, that pulled him and pulled him with terrible strength towards the black bog next to the path.

The lads could see the light that flickered across Tom's face came from the Dead Hand itself, with its rotting flesh dropping off the mouldy bones, and its dreadful fingers tightly gripping Tom's hand, as if the two hands had grown together. More and more strongly the Hand pulled, and at last Tom let go of the willow-snag, and was dragged away and off the path and, with a great shriek, maybe like a soul in hell, he was swallowed up in the darkness.

After this, the lads could scarcely say what had happened to them. The horrors came round them, and skirled and mocked them; they never harmed the lads because of their safe-keeps and their prayers, but they howled at them, and plucked at their clothing, until the poor things were mad with terror and sick with the awfulness of it.

One lad crept up the path on his hands and knee-bones

and that's how he got out of the terrible bog; another was found lying next to a water-hole; and so, one by one, the villagers who came into the marsh got them all out. But the lads were out of their wits with fear, and they couldn't bring themselves to say what had happened to Long Tom. Each time someone asked where to find him, they began to screech and sob with terror, so the villagers could get nothing out of the poor creatures that night.

The next day, though, the villagers heard all about Tom, and of course they went into the marsh in the good sunlight, and looked and looked for him. His poor mother called and cried out for him; she swore she couldn't live without her only son, her baby, and she a poor widow woman.

But the villagers couldn't find a trace of the lad. Then the women took the old mother back to her cottage, and tried to comfort her and hush her sobbing; but the poor creature tore away from them like a mad thing, and ran back to the marsh, and just as before, she began calling and calling on her son to come back to his poor lonely mother, and she a widow.

Over and over again the old woman cried out and wailed for her son, and the villagers could do nothing to hush her. So they had to leave her be, for they could find not a trace of Long Tom.

As the days passed by, people went back to work; the boys who had followed Tom into the marsh began to creep about, scared and white and trembling; then you might have thought things were much the same as they had been before. But Tom didn't come back. And night after night the lamp flared in the window of the cottage at the end of the lane, and the old woman sat up waiting for her boy, and the door stood open from sundown until dawn. And all day long, the old woman wandered along the marsh paths, calling and calling on her son to come back, come back to his mother, and she a widow!

The village people were kind of afraid of the old woman, and kept out of her way when she came past. She was so grey and bent and wrinkled and sorrowful, and flitted about like one of the bog-things themselves.

So the days wore on, and it was the seventh evening since Tom had been dragged into the marsh. Some of the villagers were sauntering along the edge of the marsh, as they had taken to doing since the lad had been lost, when all at once, just before dark, they heard a great cry – and a second great cry, so full of wonder and joy it was sort of gruesome to hear it. And as they stood there, waiting and wondering, they saw the old mother scurrying towards them along one of the marsh-paths, beckoning and waving like mad.

It was a bit scary, but nonetheless the villagers followed her out into the marsh, as fast as their bones would carry them. They caught up with her at the willow-snag – and there sat Long Tom with his back against the stump, and his feet in the water! There he sat, with his mother sobbing over him, and kissing every inch of him. But my faith! What a changed creature he was! His back was bent, his limbs were shaking like an old grandfather, his great blazing eyes glared out of a white wrinkled face, and his hair, once so brown and curly, was white and grey and hanging down in long straggling wisps.

With one hand, Tom kept pointing, pointing at something, and staring at something, as if he could see nothing else; and where the other hand ought to have been, the hand gripped by the dreadful Dead Fingers, there was nothing but a ragged, bleeding stump – Tom's hand had been pulled clean off!

There he sat, gibbering and grinning, grinning at the horrors, which nobody but himself could see! Ah! And no one ever did know just what he could see, and what he had seen during those awful nights and days which he spent with the horrors; no one ever knew where he had been, or how he had come back, except what that bleeding stump told them of a terrible struggle with the awful Hand, a tugging for dear life. For after they found him by the snag, with his mother crooning over him and fondling him, Long Tom Pattison never spoke another word.

All day long he would sit in the sun, or sit by the fire, grinning and grinning; and all night long he wandered beside the edge of the marsh, screeching and moaning like a thing in torment, with his poor old mother tagging along like a dog at heel, begging and praying him to come home. And when one of Tom's old friends stopped by to have a look at him, Tom's mother would pat the silly poor creature's head and say: 'He said he'd come home, and he did; my baby did come to his mother, and she a widow woman.'

That's all there is to it. It's not much of a story – but as you can see, it was all a result of Tom's disbelieving ways. The poor creature didn't live for more than a year. When he died, the village women took his mother away from his corpse, and tried their best to stop her from going back to him; but when they came to put the lad into his coffin for the funeral, there she was, propped up in one corner of the bed, with Tom in her arms. She was nursing him as she used to do when he was a little thing, and she was dead – dead – like her son lying across her knees.

People said the old woman was smiling like a sleeping baby; but on Tom's face – ah! there was an awful look, as if the horrors had followed him and fought to have him for themselves.

Long Tom couldn't rest in his grave in the churchyard, and on dark nights before the marsh was drained, he went moaning up and down along the edge of the bog, with his old mother trailing after him. And through the shrieking and sobbing, people said they could hear the old woman's voice, whimpering and calling out, as she'd done so often in life: 'He came back to his mother, he did, and she a widow woman.'

Close to the town of Bures, near
Sudbury, there has lately appeared, to
the great hurt of the countryside, a
dragon, vast in body, with a crested
head, teeth like a saw, and a tail
extending to an enormous length.
Having slaughtered the shepherd of a
flock, it devoured many sheep. There
came forth in order to shoot at him
with arrows the workmen of the lord on
whose estate he had concealed himself,
being Sir Richard de Waldegrave,
Knight; but the dragon's body,
although struck by the archers,
remained unhurt, for the arrows

bounced off his back as if it were iron or
hard rock. Those arrows that fell upon
the spine of his back gave out as they
struck it a ringing or tinkling sound,
just as if they had hit a brazen plate,
and then flew away off by reason of the
hide of this great beast being
impenetrable. Thereupon, in order to
destroy him, all the country people
around were summoned. But when the
dragon saw that he was again about to
be assailed with arrows, he fled into a
marsh or mere and there hid himself
among the long reeds, and was no more
seen.

HENRY DE BLANEFORD

Shonks and
the Dragon

✣

'Me?' said the Lord of the Manor of Pelham. 'You,' said his daughter, namely Miss Eleanor. 'You've no choice.'

The Lord of the Manor, alias Sir Piers Shonks, crossed the huge trunk of his left leg over the huge trunk of his right leg, and sighed terribly. He stared into the fire until his eyeballs were burning.

'Mmm!' he said.

'Think of Sigurd and Beowulf and Carantoc!' exclaimed Eleanor.

'Tittle-tattle!' said Shonks.

'Assipattle, you mean,' said Eleanor.

'Prittle-prattle,' muttered her father.

'And now,' exclaimed Eleanor, 'Sir Piers Shonks!'

'Shonks, conks, honks,' said the Lord of the Manor of Pelham. 'Does it sound as if I'm a dragon-slayer?'

'Brave men need dragons,' Eleanor said, and there were dragons dancing in her eyes.

'I don't need a dragon,' said Shonks. 'No, thank you.'

'You do,' said Eleanor. 'To prove yourself. Anyhow, you've got no choice.'

'I have!' said Shonks.

'You've no choice in the matter,' Eleanor repeated. 'You're the Lord of the Manor and he's the dragon of Brent Pelham. You've got to fight him.'

✤

The Lord of the Manor had a difficult dream. He had decided once and for all not to fight the dragon. 'Dragons be blowed!' he could hear himself saying. 'Dragons be blowed be blasted be Brummagemmed . . .'

But then the dragon of Brent Pelham came visiting. It shrithed into the manor and, most mysteriously, seemed to turn into his daughter, so that whenever Shonks looked at Eleanor, he seemed to be looking at the dragon.

And then, even more strangely, Shonks dreamt he was turning into the dragon himself. He was becoming a wrong-doer, an evil flame-thrower, and the very people who depended on him now began to avoid him.

So when Shonks woke up, sweating and cold, after a horrible argument with his sheets and blankets, he knew his daughter was right. He had no choice! In the name of every man, woman and child living in Brent Pelham – why! in his own name, modest as it was – he had to fight the dragon.

'Brute!' said Shonks, most miserably. 'Biggonet, bastion, blabber, bodily, bone-white . . .' On and on he went, as if he were a walking lexicon. But quite what he was talking about is impossible to tell.

✤

If anything, Sir Piers Shonks' armour was even more reluctant than its owner. It had long since gone into retirement; its shoulders and elbows and knees and ankles creaked and cracked, and for year after year armies of clothes-moths had picnicked in the woollen padding inside the helmet.

'Darn!' grumbled Shonks. And then, 'Drat! Devil's teeth!'

'Courage!' said Eleanor, helping her father secure his sword-belt.

'That's what you're going to need, my girl,' said Shonks.

'Me?' said Eleanor.

'I'm taking you with me.'

Eleanor's eyes opened sky-wide.

'You're the best man I've got,' said her father. 'Anyhow, I'm between squires.'

So while the armourer oiled Shonks' groaning joints and the blacksmith stropped his sword and spear, Eleanor stepped upstairs and changed into the best dress in her garderobe.

'And now for my snood,' she said. 'Snood! I hate that word.'

✜

The dragon had made a mess of Brent Pelham. He had set fire to two of the embattled old oaks, guardians of the village green since the days of King Alfred. He had flattened whole hedgerows. And worst of all, he had knocked down seven little cruck-cottages, eaten three harvest-heavy pigs and dozens of chickens, and blown out the new nativity window at the east end of the church.

'Blessed Virgin preserve me!' said Shonks.

'She's nothing but glass splinters,' Eleanor said. 'All over the churchyard. You'll have to make do with the saints. Saint Martha and Saint George. Philip and Pol.'

Father and daughter galloped along the ride between Great Pepsells and Little Pepsells, and Shonks' three best hounds galloped beside them – and all three were so fleet and light of foot that one old man, rather the worse for wear, was quite certain they had wings. In both fields, the poor corn looked as if it had run this way and run that way and pressed its ears to the ground . . .

And underground, in its lair beneath the roots of the great yew tree, the dragon heard them coming. It rose to the light.

'Dear God!' said Shonks. And then, 'BACK! BACK!' he shouted at Eleanor. 'My beautiful! Brightest! Best! My everything else beginning with B!'

Then Shonks dismounted and he and the dragon joined battle. Shonks raised his ashen spear and the dragon raised its head. It bellowed, it blew out vile sulphurous smoke.

Many is the battle won by mistake. When the dragon threw fire at him, Shonks stepped sideways to avoid the jet-stream; he stepped and tripped and fell forward; and falling, he thrust his spear right down the dragon's throat.

'Aargh!' said the dragon.

Gargle and spit! Humans, horses, hounds – and all the birds in heaven itself – were coated with flecks of pink foam. It made the three hounds grin and sneeze.

'Listen to the birds!' shouted Shonks. 'Life! That's what they're singing. Lifelife. Life!'

'Father,' called Eleanor. Quickly she dismounted, then she picked up her skirts, ran towards Shonks over the bumpy ground, and threw herself into his metal embrace.

✧

When Sir Piers and Miss Eleanor had disentangled themselves, they saw a man leaning quite nonchalantly against one side of the dead dragon.

'Good morning!' he said, and he smiled and blew on his long white fingers. He was very slight, and his hair and eyes were both dark. 'Good morning to you both!'

'Where have you come from?' asked Shonks.

'Immediately,' said the man, 'from Cambridge. Or do you mean, how did I get here?'

'Well,' said Shonks, 'I haven't seen you around here before.'

'No,' said the man, still smiling, and he flexed his fingers. 'I live in your hereafter.'

'My hereafter?'

'So we should be seeing plenty of one another before too long.'

'What do you mean?' asked Eleanor, and she took her father's arm. 'What's your name?'

'I have many names,' said the little man quite affably. 'Some say, the *great dragon*.'

'I know my Book of Revelation,' said Shonks quickly. 'I know who you are.'

'Then you know why I'm here,' said the man.

'Saint Matthew and Saint Mark and Saint Luke and Saint John,' murmured Shonks. 'May they trample the dragon under their feet!'

'I see you've killed my servant,' said the little man. 'Well! A life for a life! You've killed the dragon of Brent Pelham; so when you die, Piers Shonks, I'll have you.'

'No!' cried Shonks. 'Not! Never! Numquam!'

'Oh yes, Shonks. I'll have you, body and soul.'

'Not if I'm buried inside the church. I'll have them bury me inside the church.'

'Inside the church, outside the church, it doesn't matter to me, I'll have you either way.'

'Never!' shouted Shonks again.

The man winked at Miss Eleanor. 'And you, my pretty,' he said, 'you're my witness.'

Piers Shonks shook off one of his gauntlets and bowed his head and crossed himself. 'I commend my soul to God,' he said. 'And when I die, my body will lie – lie undisturbed and sleep – exactly where I choose.'

The man arched his black eyebrows and smiled at Shonks. There were flames in his freezing eyes. Then he simply stamped one foot and disappeared.

❖

Years passed and Sir Piers Shonks became old. He became very old and his mouth grew dry.

'Dreary, devil, dragon, dropsical, Dunstable,' muttered Shonks as he lay on his death-bed. 'And everything else beginning with D.' And then, rallying himself considerably, 'Carry me outside! Bring me my longbow!'

Six manor servants lifted the Lord of the Manor of Pelham, still lying on his bed. They carried him down to the moat, and there Miss Eleanor put his longbow in his speckled hands.

'Cut from the great yew – the one between Great Pepsells and Little Pepsells,' said Eleanor. 'Do you remember, father?'

'Oh, do shut up!' said Shonks. 'Give me an arrow!'

Shonks screwed up his eyes and drew in his lips and notched an arrow.

'Now listen to me!' he said. 'I'll shoot this one arrow and then I'll die.'

The manor servants began to get down on their knees in the wet grass.

'Bury me wherever this arrow falls! Wherever it falls. Do you understand me?'

The six servants nodded.

'As you choose, father,' said Miss Eleanor.

'Inside or outside, indeed!' grumbled Shonks. 'Inside the church, outside the church, I'll show him.'

Then the Lord of the Manor of Pelham summoned up all the remaining strength in his body. He drew back the bowstring as far as he could, and then even a little further, and released it.

The string hummed and shuddered and fell still, but the arrow flew singing through the bright air. It rose and sped and dipped, dipped and stuck into the north wall of Brent Pelham church.

✢

So Shonks died smiling. Not inside the church, not outside the church: he was buried deep within the church wall. The devil reached out his long white fingers and he still could not touch him.

Well now I will try and tell how
the poacher work. There are many
ways of taking phesants and other
game, the gun, the hingle or snare,
the trap, and the net. Wen the
poacher enter a wood as I have said
befor he goes with the wind in his
face, as phesants always sit facen
the wind, to keep there feathers
down. He draws along as quietly as
possible till he se his bird, then crall
with in shot of it and kill it.

Years ago we used to use a sight of
this kind. Cut a pair of ears out of a
stuff pice of leather and use it on the
muzzle of the gun – so it look like
rabbits ears on the end . . . The snare is

used were the phesants creep through hedges, a bow stick being put round the hingle to make the bird drop his head. Another way is to make a hole in the ground three inch deep and two inch across the top. The hingle is laid round the hole that have already been partly filled with white peas. He come along and put his head in the hole, bring the hingle up on his neck and is verry sone dead.

GEORGE BALDRY

The Devil Take the Hindmost

'Midnight, then,' said Mace. George Mace. He glared at his two companions, then sniffed and drank off the rest of his beer, 'Breckles Hall. You know where.'

Almost at once two more men got up from a table on the other side of the bar, and sauntered over to him. As if he were a magnet and they were two poor pins.

'Midnight,' Mace repeated. 'The Hall. You know where.' He stood up and stretched, like a giant bat reaching right over them. 'And the devil take the hindmost,' he added. Slowly he coiled a piece of snaring-wire round the lowest button of his greatcoat. Then he walked out into the January night.

The four men looked at one another and looked into their glasses of beer.

'The devil take the hindmost,' muttered one man.

'He can go to the devil himself,' the second man said. 'Mace.'

'That's what he deserves,' the third man said.

'And that's what he'll get,' said the fourth.

There was something dark and chancy about Mace. He was deep as drowning water, and dangerous as thin ice.

'You never know where you stand with him.'

'He'll mother a stray kitten.'

'And stab his own mother.'

That's what people said.

Everyone in Watton muttered and complained about Mace behind his back, but no one criticised him to his face. No one crossed him or riled him; no, they did as he ordered them, because they were afraid of what might happen otherwise. No one went out alone with Mace, though, not since he and Bobby Cossey had gone shooting near the sandpits, and only Mace had come back.

Mace's companions were nervous about their night's work, and they were uneasy about Breckles Hall: they knew about the phantom coach and its dark driver; and they'd heard about the Catholic priests in cramped priestholes, the Protestants with burning eyes and burning brands, ferreting them out; miserable suicides; and a mad woman entombed upright inside one wall. But the truth is, the four men were even more nervous of their leader. Each left his cottage in good time and they were all wearing sombre clothing: midnight blue jerseys, charcoal jackets, moleskin trousers, dun coats with wide pockets – nothing that could wink at the moon.

One man was carrying a snare, and another a grinning ferret; one had a couple of flams – little purse-nets; the fourth was carrying on his shoulder an ugly-looking trap; and each man had a hempen sack.

Mace was waiting for them under the great oak in the middle of the little wood in front of Breckles Hall.

'That's a shiny night,' said one man with satisfaction.

Mace gave a kind of nod – an upward thrust of his chin.

'They're thumping in their burrows,' he said.

Midnight and the wood was far from silent, for those with ears to hear such things. The poachers put their heads to the ground and listened to the rabbits running around their warrens. They heard the creak-creak of the pheasant and the oo-hoo of the barn owl. Mace was so sharp he could have heard a hare pricking up its ears.

'Right!' he said. 'Two and two. I'll work on my own. I'll work with the devil!'

'Fred and me,' said one man. 'The old team.'

'Who's running this show?' said Mace quietly.

The four men murmured.

'You all got wire?'

Again the men murmured. 'Right! Laddie and Bill, you do the pheasants and the partridge. Fred! You and Martin do rabbit and hare. Five o'clock we'll meet in the gardener's shed – you know, behind the Hall.'

'Five o'clock,' said the men.

'And settle up,' said Mace, 'before the moon goes down. Five o'clock. And the devil take the hindmost.'

That was a fine night's work. One of the very best. Pheasants and partridges and rabbits and hares! They fell into the flams and snares as if there were no tomorrow. And for them that did, there wasn't!

By five o'clock, Laddie and Bill and Fred and Martin had so much game in their sacks they could scarcely carry them to the shed behind the Hall. Indeed, Bill dragged his sack behind him, and it scored a track through the shining hoar-frost.

But where was Mace? Where was he?

'That's not like him,' muttered Bill. 'Not at all, that isn't.'

The four men huddled in the shed. Inside was even colder than outside, and for the first time that night Jack Frost stole up on them. He crept in and tweaked their noses; he pinched the lobes of their ears, and pincered their fingertips and nipped their toes. Then he showed his white teeth.

The moon sank. First it hung on the skyline, then it disappeared. After this, the darkness was intense. The kind of darkness that makes a man wonder what shape he is, and even whether he exists.

'What shall we do?' said one man in a low voice.

'Damn him!'

'Come on! Let's settle up!'

'Listen!' said Fred. 'Listen!'

First it was far-off, like a sound in your memory. Then it grew closer and began to rumble, but not like thunder. Not as grand as that. And then the sound rolled and crunched and cracked. Coach wheels rolling over gravel, slowly rolling up to the front of the Hall.

The four poachers peered through the door of the shed, and saw swinging lights in the back windows of the Hall.

'That's them coach-lamps,' muttered Fred. 'Shining in through the front windows and out through the back.'

That's just what it was. And now the lamps stopped swinging and the stained glass in the Hall's back windows threw patterns and patches of colour out across the frosty lawn in front of the poachers. Freezing blue. Grey-green, sickly as dawn. Scarlet, bright as rabbits' blood.

A creak and then a thump.

'That's the coach steps,' Laddie whispered.

Another creak. And then the slam of the coach door.

The four men listened for the coach to roll away again. But there was not a sound. Not the sound of a voice; not the crack of a whip. The lamps were out. The coach vanished. And if any of the men had been in the shed on his own, he would have thought he'd imagined it all.

'Home!' said Laddie hoarsely.

'Each man his own sack!'

As the men hurried to get home before dawn, they kept wondering about Mace. Where he was. What had happened to him. And they thought about the phantom coach.

Next morning, Mace was found. He had been dumped on the doorstep of Breckles Hall. His body was not marked and his clothes were not bloodstained. His eyes were open and staring and glassy and cold.

1 Unna   6 Hater
2 Tina   7 Skater
3 Wether   8 Sara
4 Tether   9 Dara
5 Pinkie   10 Dick

TRADITIONAL (SUFFOLK SHEPHERDS)

Tom Tit Tot

✛

There was once a little old village where a woman lived with her giddy daughter. The daughter was just sixteen, and sweet as honeysuckle.

One fine morning, the woman made five meat pies and put them in the oven. But then a neighbour called round and they were soon so busy gossiping that the woman forgot about the pies. By the time she took them out of the oven, their crusts were as hard as the bark of her old oak tree.

'Daughter,' she says, 'you put them there pies in the larder.'

'My! I'm that hungry,' says the girl.

'Leave them there and they'll come again,' says the woman. And what she meant, you know, was that the crusts would get soft.

'Well!' the girl says to herself, 'if they'll come again, I'll eat

these ones now.' And so she set to work and ate them all, first and last.

When it was supper time, the woman felt very hungry.

'I could just do with one of them there pies,' she says.

'Go and get one off the shelf. They'll have come again by now.'

The girl went and looked, but there was nothing on the shelf except an empty dish. 'No!' she calls. 'They haven't.'

'Not none of them?' says the woman.

'No!' calls the girl. 'No! Not none.'

'Well!' says the woman. 'Come again or not, I'll have one for my supper.'

'You can't if they haven't come,' says the girl.

'I can though,' says the woman. 'Go and get the best one.'

'Best or worst,' says the girl, 'I've eaten the lot, so you can't have one until it's come again.'

The woman was furious. 'Eaten the lot? You dardle-dum-due!'

The woman carried her spinning wheel over to the door and to calm herself, she began to spin. As she spun she sang:

> *'My daughter's ate five; five pies today.*
> *My daughter's ate five; five pies today.'*

The king came walking down the street and heard the woman.

'What were those words, woman?' he says. 'What were you singing?'

The woman felt ashamed of her daughter's greed. 'Well!' she says, beginning to spin again:

> *'My daughter's spun five; five skeins today.*
> *My daughter's spun five; five skeins today.'*

'Stars of mine!' exclaims the king. 'I've never heard of any-one who could do that.' The king raised his eyebrows and looked at the girl, so sweet and giddy and sixteen.

'Five today,' says the woman.

'Look here!' says the king. 'I want a wife and I'll marry your daughter. For eleven months of the year,' he says, 'she can eat as much food as she likes, and buy all the dresses she wants; she can keep whatever company she wishes. But during the last month of the year, she'll have to spin five skeins every day; and if she doesn't, I'll cut off her head.'

'All right!' says the woman. 'That's all right, isn't it, daughter?'

The woman was delighted at the thought that her daughter was going to marry the king himself. She wasn't worried about the five skeins. 'When that comes to it,' she said to her daughter later, 'we'll find a way out of it. More likely, though, he'll have clean forgotten about it.'

So the king and the girl were married. And for eleven months the girl ate as much food as she liked and bought all the dresses she wanted and kept whatever company she wished.

As the days of the eleventh month passed, the girl began to think about those skeins and wondered whether the king was thinking about them too. But the king said not a word, and the girl was quite sure he had forgotten them.

On the very last day of the month, though, the king led her up to a room in the palace she had never set eyes on before. There was nothing in it but a spinning wheel and a stool.

'Now, my dear,' says the king, 'you'll be shut in here tomorrow with some food and some flax. And if you haven't spun five skeins before dark, your head will be cut off.'

Then away went the king to do everything a king has to do.

Well, the girl was that frightened. She had always been such a giddy girl, and she didn't know how to spin. She didn't know what to do next morning, with no one beside her and no one to help her. She sat down on a stool in the palace kitchen and heavens! how she did cry.

All of a sudden, however, she heard a sort of knocking low down on the door. So she stood up and opened it, and what did she see but a small little black thing with a long tail. That looked up at her, all curious, and that said, 'What are you crying for?'

'What's that to you?' says the girl.

'Never you mind,' that says. 'You tell me what you're crying for.'

'That won't do me no good if I do,' the girl replies.

'You don't know that,' that said, and twirled its tail round.

'Well!' she says. 'That won't do me no harm if that don't do me no good.' So she told him about the pies and the skeins and everything.

'This is what I'll do,' says the little black thing. 'I'll come to your window every morning and take the flax; and I'll bring it back all spun before dark.'

'What will that cost?' she asks.

The thing looked out of the corners of its eyes and said, 'Every night I'll give you three guesses at my name. And if you haven't guessed it before the month's up, you shall be mine.'

The girl thought she was bound to guess its name before the month was out. 'All right!' she says. 'I agree to that.'

'All right!' that says, and lork! how that twirled that's tail.

Well, next morning, the king led the girl up to the room, and the flax and the day's food were all ready for her.

'Now there's the flax,' he says. 'And if it isn't spun before dark, off goes your head!' Then he went out and locked the door.

The king had scarcely gone out when there was a knocking at the window.

The girl stood up and opened it and sure enough, there was the little old thing sitting on the window ledge.

'Where's the flax?' it says.

'Here you are!' she says. And she gave it the flax.

When it was early evening, there was a knocking again at the window. The girl stood up and opened it, and there was the little old thing, with five skeins over its arm.

'Here you are!' that says, and it gave the flax to her. 'And now,' it says, 'what's my name?'

'What, is that Bill?' she says.

'No!' it says, 'that ain't.' And that twirled that's tail.

'Is that Ned?' she says.

'No!' it says, 'that ain't.' And that twirled that's tail.

'Well, is that Mark?' says she.

'No!' it says, 'that ain't.' And that twirled that's tail faster, and away it flew.

When the girl's husband came in, the five skeins were ready for him. 'I see I shan't have to kill you tonight, my dear,' he says. 'You'll have your food and your flax in the morning,' he says, and away he went to do everything a king has to do.

Well, the flax and the food were made ready for the girl each day, and each day the little black impet used to come in the morning and return in the early evening. And each day and all day the girl sat thinking of names to try out on the impet when it came back in the evening. But she never hit on the right one! As time went on towards the end of the month, the impet looked wickeder and wickeder, and that twirled that's tail faster and faster each time she made a guess.

So they came to the last day of the month but one. The impet returned in the early evening with the five skeins, and it said, 'What, hain't you guessed my name yet?'

'Is that Nicodemus?' she says.

'No! 't'ain't,' that says.

'Is that Samuel?' she says.

'No! 't'ain't,' that says.

'Ah well! Is that Methusalem?' says she.

'No! 't'ain't that either,' it says. And then that looks at the girl with eyes like burning coals.

'Woman,' that says, 'there's only tomorrow evening, and then you'll be mine!' And away it flew!

Well, the girl felt terrible. Soon, though, she heard the king coming along the passage; and when he had walked into the room and seen the five skeins, he says, 'Well, my dear! So far as I can see, you'll have your skeins ready tomorrow evening too. I reckon I won't have to kill you, so I'll have my supper in here tonight.' Then the king's servants brought up his supper, and another stool for him, and the two of them sat down together.

The king had scarcely eaten a mouthful before he pushed back his stool, and waved his knife and fork, and began to laugh.

'What is it?' asks the girl.

'I'll tell you,' says the king. 'I was out hunting today, and I got lost and came to a clearing in the forest I'd never seen before. There was an old chalkpit there. And I heard a kind of sort of humming. So I got off my horse and crept up to the edge of the pit and looked down. And do you know what I saw? The funniest little black thing you ever set eyes on! And what did that have but a little spinning wheel! That was spinning and spinning, wonderfully fast, spinning and twirling that's tail. And as it spun, it sang,

> *'Nimmy nimmy not,*
> *My name's Tom Tit Tot.'*

Well, when the girl heard this, she felt as if she could have jumped out of her skin for joy; but she didn't say a word.

Next morning, the small little black thing looked wicked as

wicked when it came for the flax. And just before it grew dark, she heard it knocking again at the window pane. She opened the window and that came right in on to the sill. It was grinning from ear to ear, and ooh! that's tail was twirling round so fast.

'What's my name?' that says, as it gave her the skeins.

'Is that Solomon?' she says, pretending to be afraid.

'No! 't'ain't,' that says, and it came further into the room.

'Well, is that Zebedee?' she says again.

'No! 't'ain't,' says the impet. And then that laughed and twirled that's tail until you could scarcely see it.

'Take time, woman,' that says. 'Next guess, and you're mine.' And that stretched out its black hands towards her.

The girl backed away a step or two. She looked at it, and then she laughed and pointed a finger at it and sang out:

> *'Nimmy nimmy not,*
> *Your name's Tom Tit Tot.'*

Well! When the impet heard her, that gave an awful shriek and away it flew into the dark. She never saw it again.

'Life is sweet, brother.'
'Do you think so?'
'Think so! There's night and day,
brother, both sweet things; sun,
moon and stars, brother, all sweet
things; there's likewise a wind on the
heath. Life is very sweet, brother;
who would wish to die?'

GEORGE BORROW

The Gipsy Woman

a sequel to 'Tom Tit Tot'

✤

Now then! The girl ate well and dressed well and enjoyed the best of company for the whole of the next year, until the eleventh month was almost over.

And then her husband says to her: 'Well, my dear, today's the end of the month. Tomorrow you'll have to begin again, and spin your five skeins every day.'

The girl thought her husband had clean forgotten about the skeins, and now she didn't know what to do. She knew she couldn't count on Tom Tit Tot again, and she couldn't spin a mite herself: and so her head would have to come off!

Poor Toad, she sat herself down on a stool in the bake-

house, and she cried as if her heart would break.

All at once, the girl heard someone knocking at the door. So she got up and unlocked it, and there stood a gipsy woman, as brown as a berry.

'Well, well! What's all this to-do?' she says. 'What are you crying like that for?'

'Get away, you gipsy woman,' says she. 'Don't you poke your nose in where you're no use.'

'Tell me what's wrong, and maybe I *shall* be some use,' says the woman. And she looked so understanding that the girl stood up and told her.

'Is that all?' she says. 'I've helped people out of worse holes than this, and now I'll help you.'

'Ah! But what will you ask for helping me?' says the girl, for she was thinking of how she'd almost given herself away to the bad-tempered little black impet.

'I don't want anything except the best suit of clothes you have got,' says the gipsy.

'You shall have them, and welcome,' says the girl, and she ran and opened the chest where her best dresses and things were, and gave one to the woman, and a brooch of gay gold. For she thought to herself, 'If she's a cheat and can't help me, and my head is cut off, it won't matter if I *have* given away my best gown.'

The woman was delighted when she saw the gown. 'Now then!' she says, 'you'll have to ask all the people you know to a damned fine party, and I'll come to it.'

Well, the girl went to her husband, and she says: 'My dear, seeing as this is the last night before I spin, I should like to have a party.'

'All right, my dear,' he says.

So the people were all asked, and they came in their best clothes: silks and satins, and all manner of fine things.

Well, they all had a grand supper with the best of foods,

and they enjoyed themselves a great deal. But the gipsy woman never came near them, and the girl's heart was in her mouth.

One of the lords, who was tired of dancing, said it wasn't long off bull's noon, and it was time to go.

'No, no! Stay a little longer,' the girl says. 'Let's have a game of blind man's bluff first.' So they began to play.

Just then the door flew open, and in came the gipsy woman. She'd washed herself, and combed her hair, and wound a gay handkerchief round her head, and put on the grand gown, so that she looked like a queen.

'Stars of mine!' says the king. 'Who's that?'

'Oh! That's a friend of mine,' says the girl. And she watched to see what the gipsy would do.

'What, are you playing blind man's bluff?' says the gipsy. 'I'll join in with you.'

And so she did. But what was in her pocket but a little pot of cold cart-grease? And as she ran around, she dipped her hand in this grease, and smudged it on people as she brushed past them.

That wasn't long before someone cried out. 'O lord! There's some nasty stuff on my gown.'

'Why, it's on my dress too,' says another. 'That must have come off you.'

'No! That it didn't! You've put it on me.' And then almost everyone began to shout and quarrel, each one thinking someone else had gone and smirched them.

Then the king stepped forward and listened to the hullaballoo. The ladies were crying, and the gentlemen were shouting, and all their fine clothes were daubed with grease.

'Why, what's this?' he says, for there was a great mark on the sleeve of his coat. He smelt it and turned up his nose. 'That's cart-grease,' he says.

'No, it isn't,' says the gipsy woman. 'That comes off my

hand. That's spindle-grease.'

'Why, what's spindle-grease?' he says.

'Well,' she says, 'I've been a great spinner in my time, and I spun and spun and spun five skeins a day. And because I spun so much, the spindle grease worked into my hands; and now, as often as I wash them, I dirty each thing I touch. And if your wife spins as much as I do, she'll have spindle grease like I have.'

The king looked at his coat sleeve, and he rubbed it and sniffed at it and then he said to his wife: 'Look here, my dear, and listen to what I say. If ever I see you again with a spindle in your hands, your head will go off!'

So the girl never had to spin again.

And that's all.

I would say, at the risk of brick-
bats, that the Norfolker is sharp,
acquisitive and distrustful of
strangers. A good friend when he
knows you.

The Suffolker is slower, kinder,
gentler in speech and manner, not
nearly so smart in business but not
such a fool as others think he is.

The Fenman is tall, thin, dark,
frequently with high cheek bones
and an eagle-beak – the long-
descended characteristics of his
Jutish forebears with, perhaps,
even a mystic throw-back to the
dark, athletic tribesmen of the
Girvii and Caritavi who dwelt

on the Fen isles of reed and willow
and paddled their dug-out canoes
long before the Saxons came. Too
often the Fenman is uncouth,
cunning, pugnacious, and hates
strangers. You must have lived
there for centuries to be accepted.

J. WENTWORTH DAY

The Dead Moon

✥

Long ago, the moon used to shine just as she shone last night. And when she shone, she cast her light over the marshland: the great pools of black water, and the creeping trickles of green water, and the squishy mounds that sucked anyone in who stepped on them. She lit up the whole swamp so that people could walk about almost as safely as in broad daylight.

But when the moon did not shine, out came the Things that live in the darkness. They wormed around, waiting for a chance to harm those people who were not safe at home beside their own hearths. Harm and mishap and evil: bogles and dead things and crawling horrors: they all appeared on the nights when the moon did not shine.

The moon came to hear of this. And being kind and good, as she surely is, shining for us night after night instead of going to sleep, she was upset at what was going on behind her back. She said to herself, 'I'll see what's going on for myself. Maybe it's not as bad as people make out.'

And sure enough, at the end of the month the moon stepped down on to the earth, wearing a black cloak and black hood over her yellow shining hair. She went straight to the edge of the bogland and looked about her.

There was water here, and water there; waving tussocks, trembling mounds, and great black snags of peat all twisted and bent; and in front of her, everything was dark – dark except for the pools glimmering under the stars and the light that came from the moon's own white feet, poking out beneath her black cloak.

The moon walked forward, right into the middle of the marsh, always looking to left and to right, and over her shoulders. Then she saw she had company, and strange company at that.

'Witches,' whispered the moon, and the witches grinned at her as they rode past on their huge black cats.

'The eye,' she whispered, and the evil eye glowered at her from the deepest darkness.

'Will-o'-the-wykes,' whispered the moon, and the will-o'-the-wykes danced around her with their lanterns swinging on their backs.

'The dead,' she whispered, and dead folk rose out of the water. Their faces were white and twisted and hell-fire blazed in their empty eye sockets, and they stared blindly round them.

'And dead hands,' whispered the moon. Slimy dripping dead hands slithered about, beckoning and pointing, so cold and wet that they made the moon's skin crawl.

The moon drew her cloak more tightly around her and

trembled. But she was resolved not to go back without seeing all there was to be seen. So on she went, stepping as lightly as the summer wind from tuft to tuft between the greedy gurgling water holes.

Just as the moon came up to a big black pool, her foot slipped. With both hands she grabbed at a snag of peat to steady herself, and save herself from tumbling in. But as soon as she touched it, the snag twined itself round her wrists like a pair of handcuffs, and gripped her so that she couldn't escape. The moon pulled and twisted and fought, but it was no good; she was trapped, completely trapped. Then she looked about her, and wondered if anyone at all would be out that night, and pass by, and help her. But she saw nothing except shifting, flurrying evil Things, coming and going, to-ing and fro-ing, all of them busy and all of them up to no good.

After a while, as the moon stood trembling in the dark, she heard something calling in the distance – a voice that called and called, and then died away in a sob. Then the voice was raised again in a screech of pain and fear, and called and called, until the marshes were haunted by that pitiful crying sound. Then the moon heard the sound of steps, someone floundering along, squishing through the mud, slipping on the tufts. And, through the darkness, she saw a pair of hands catching at the snags and tussocks, and a white face with wide, terrified eyes.

It was a man who had strayed into the marsh. The grinning bogles and dead folk and creeping horrors crawled and crowded around him; voices mocked him; the dead hands plucked at him. And, ahead of him, the will-o'-the-wykes dangled their lanterns, and shook with glee as they lured him further and further away from the safe path over the swamp. Trembling with fear and loathing at the Things all around him, the man struggled on towards the flickering lights ahead of him that looked as if they would give him help and bring him home in safety.

'You over there!' yelled the man. 'You! I'm caught in the swamp. Can you hear me?' His voice rose to a shriek. 'Help! You over there! Help! God and Mary save me from these horrors!' Then the man paused, and sobbed and moaned, and called on the saints and wise women and on God Himself to save him from the swamp.

But then the man shrieked again as the slimy slithery Things crawled around him and reared up so that he could not even see the false lights, the will-o'-the-wykes, ahead of him.

As if matters were not bad enough already, the horrors began to take on all sorts of shapes: beautiful girls winked at him with their bright eyes, and stretched out soft helping hands towards him. But when he tried to catch hold of them, they changed in his grip to slimy things and shapeless worms, and evil voices derided him and mocked him with foul laughter. Then all the bad thoughts that the man had ever had, and all the bad things that he had ever done, came and whispered in his ears, and danced about, and shouted out all the secrets that were buried in his own heart. The man shrieked and sobbed with pain and with shame, and the horrors crawled and gibbered around him and mocked him.

When the poor moon saw that the man was getting nearer and nearer to the deep water holes and deadly sinking mud, and further and further from firm ground, she was so angry and so sorry for him that she struggled and fought and pulled harder than ever. She still couldn't break loose. But with all her twisting and tugging, her black hood fell back from her shining yellow hair. And the beautiful light that came from it drove away the darkness.

The man cried for joy to see God's own light again. And at

once the evil Things, unable to stand the light, scurried and delved and dropped away into their dark corners. They left the man and fled. And the man could see where he was, and where the path was, and which way to take to get out of the marsh.

He was in such a hurry to get away from the sinking mud and the swamp, and all the Things that lived there, that he scarcely glanced at the brave light that shone from the beautiful shining yellow hair streaming out over the black cloak, and falling into the water at his very feet.

And the moon herself was so taken up with saving the man, and so happy that he was back on the right path, that she completely forgot she needed help herself. For she was still trapped in the clutches of the black snag.

The man made off, gasping and stumbling and exhausted, sobbing for joy, running for his life out of the terrible swamp. Then the moon realised how much she would have liked to go with him. She shook with terror. And she pulled and fought as if she were mad, until, worn out with tugging, she fell to her knees at the foot of the snag. As the moon lay there, panting, the black hood fell forward over her head. And although she tried to toss it back again, it caught in her hair and would not move.

Out went that beautiful light, and back came the darkness with all its evil creatures, screeching and howling. They crowded around the moon, mocking at her and snatching at her and striking her; shrieking with rage and spite; swearing with foul mouths, spitting and snarling. They knew she was their old enemy, the brave bright moon, who drove them back into their corners and stopped them from doing all their wicked deeds. They swarmed all around her and made a ghastly clapperdatch. The poor moon crouched in the mud, trembling and sick at heart, and wondered when they would make an end of their caterwauling, and an end of her.

'Damn you!' yelled the witches. 'You've spoiled our spells all this last year.'

'And you keep us in our narrow coffins at night,' moaned the dead folk.

'And you send us off to skulk in the corners,' howled the bogles.

Then all the Things shouted in one voice, 'Ho, ho! Ho, ho!'

The tussocks shook and the water gurgled and the Things raised their voices again.

'We'll poison her – poison her!' shrieked the witches.

'Ho, ho!' howled the Things again.

'We'll smother her – smother her!' whispered the crawling horrors, and they twined themselves around her knees.

'Ho, ho!' shouted all the rest of them.

'We'll strangle her – strangle her!' screeched the dead hands, and they plucked at her throat with cold fingers.

'Ho, ho!' they all yelled again.

And the dead folk writhed and grinned all around her, and chuckled to themselves. 'We'll bury you – bury you down with us in the black earth!'

Once more they all shouted, full of spite and ill will. The poor moon crouched low, and wished she were dead and done for.

The Things of the darkness fought and squabbled over what should be done with the moon until the sky in the east paled and turned grey; it drew near to dawn. When they saw that, they were all worried that they would not have time to do their worst. They caught hold of the moon with horrid bony fingers, and laid her deep in the water at the foot of the snag.

The dead folk held her down while the bogles found a strange big stone. They rolled it right on top of her to stop her from getting up again.

Then the Things told two will-o'-the-wykes to take turns

at standing on the black snag to watch over the moon and make sure she lay safe and still. They didn't want her to get away and spoil their sport with her light, or help the poor marshmen at night to avoid the sinking mud and the water holes.

Then, as the grey light began to brighten, the shapeless Things fled into their dark corners; the dead folk crept back into the water, or crammed themselves into their coffins; and the witches went home to work their spells and curses. And the green slimy water shone in the light of dawn as if nothing, no wicked or evil creature, had ever gone near it.

There lay the poor moon, dead and buried in the marsh, until someone would set her free. And who knew even where to look for her?

✢

Days passed, nights passed, and it was time for the birth of the new moon. People put pennies in their pockets, and straw in their caps, so as to be ready for it. They looked up at the sky uneasily, for the moon was a good friend to the marsh folk, and they were only too happy when she began to wax, and the pathways were safe again, and the evil Things were driven back by her blessed light into the darkness and the water holes.

But day followed day and the new moon never rose. The nights were always dark and the evil Things were worse than ever. It was not safe at all to travel alone, and the boggarts crept and wailed round the houses of the marsh folk. They peeped through the windows and tipped the latches until the poor people had to burn candles and lamps all night to stop the horrors from crossing their thresholds and forcing their way in.

The bogles and other creatures seemed to have lost all their fear. They howled and laughed and screeched around the hamlet, as if they were trying to wake the dead themselves. The marsh folk listened, and sat trembling and shaking by their fires. They couldn't sleep or rest or put a foot out of doors, and one dark and dreary night followed another.

When days turned into weeks and the new moon still did not rise, the villagers were upset and afraid. A group of them went to the wise woman who lived in the old mill, and asked her if she could find out where the moon had gone.

The wise woman looked in the cauldron, and in the mirror, and in the Book. 'Well,' she said, 'it's queer. I can't tell you for sure what has happened to her.'

She shook her head and the marsh folk shook their heads.

'It's only dark and dead,' said the wise woman. 'You must wait a while, and let me think about it, and then maybe I'll be able to help you. If you hear of anything, any clue, come by and tell me. And,' said the wise woman, 'be sure to put a pinch of salt, a straw and a button on the doorstep each night. The horrors will never cross it then, light or no light.'

Then the marsh folk left the wise woman and the mill and went their separate ways. As the days went by, and the new moon never rose, they talked and talked. They wondered and pondered and worried and guessed, at home and in the inn and in the fields around the marshland.

One day, sitting on the great settle in the inn, a group of men were discussing the whereabouts of the moon, and another customer, a man from the far end of the marshland, smoked and listened to the talk. Suddenly this stranger sat up and slapped his knee. 'My Lord!' he said. 'I'd clean forgotten, but I reckon I know where the moon is.'

All the men sitting on the settle turned round to look at him. Then the stranger told them about how he had got lost in the marsh and how, when he was almost dead with fright, the light had shone out, and all the evil Things fled from it, and he had found the marsh-path and got home safely.

'And I was so terrified,' said the stranger, 'that I didn't really look to see where the light had come from. But I do remember it was white and soft like the moon herself.

'And this light came from something dark,' said the man, 'and was standing near a black snag in the water.' He paused and puffed at his pipe. 'I didn't really look,' he said again, 'but I think I remember a shining face and yellow hair in the middle of the dazzle. It had a sort of kind look, like the old moon herself above the marshland at night.'

At once all the men got up from the settle and went back to the wise woman. They told her everything the stranger had said. She listened and then looked once more into the cauldron and into the Book. Then she nodded. 'It's still dark,' she said, 'and I can't see anything for sure. But do as I tell you, and you can find out for yourselves. All of you must meet just before night falls. Put stones in your mouths,' said the wise woman, 'and take hazel twigs in your hands, and say never a word until you're safe home again. Then step out and fear nothing! Make your way into the middle of the marsh, until you find a coffin, a candle and a cross.' The wise woman stared at the circle of anxious faces around her. 'Then you won't be far from your moon,' she said. 'Search, and maybe you'll find her.'

The men looked at each other and scratched their heads.

'But where will we find her, mother?' asked one.

'And which of us must go?' asked another.

'And the bogles, won't they do for us?' said a third.

'Houts!' exclaimed the wise woman impatiently. 'You parcel of fools! I can tell you no more. Do as I've told you and fear nothing.' She glared at the men. 'And if you don't like my advice, stay at home. Do without your moon if that's what you want.'

The next day, at dusk, all the men in the hamlet came out

of their houses. Each had a stone in his mouth and a hazel twig in his hand, and each was feeling nervous and creepy.

Then the men stumbled and stuttered along the paths out into the middle of the marsh. It was so dark that they could see almost nothing. But they heard sighings and flusterings, and they could feel wet fingers touching them. On they went, peering about for the coffin, the candle and the cross, until they came near to the pool next to the great snag where the moon lay buried.

All at once they stopped in their tracks, quaking and shaking and scared. For there they saw the great stone, half in and half out of the water, looking for all the world like a strange big coffin. And at its head stood the black snag, stretching out its arms to make a dark gruesome cross. A little light flickered on it, like a dying candle.

The men knelt down in the mud, and crossed themselves, and said the Lord's Prayer to themselves. First they said it forwards because of the cross, and then they said it backwards, to keep the bogles away. But they mouthed it all without so much as a whisper, for they knew the evil Things would catch them if they did not do as the wise woman had told them.

Then the men shuffled to the edge of the water. They took hold of the big stone, and levered it up, and for one moment, just one moment, they saw a strange and beautiful face looking up at them, and looking so grateful, out of the black water.

But then the light came so quickly, and was so white and shining, that the men stepped back, stunned by it, and by the great angry wail raised by the fleeing horrors. And the very next minute, when they came to their senses, the men saw the full moon in the sky. She was as bright and beautiful and kind as ever, shining and smiling down at them; she showed the marsh and the marsh-paths as clearly as daylight and stole into every nook and cranny, as though she would have liked to drive the darkness and the bogles away for ever.

Then the marsh folk went home with light hearts and happy. And, ever since, the moon has shone more brightly and clearly over the marshland than anywhere else.

The spell of midsummer lies on the land. Down by the river in the shadow of the pale moon-flowered elders the shimmering heats hold the world in thrall. Time is sunk in the green dimness of the wood. The only sound from its depths is the low croon of the turtle dove, and the fledgling tits' thin, fleeting cries, as in little companies of eight and ten they slip through the oak trees in ceaseless search for grub and caterpillar. An hour filched from a fairy-tale, when fantasy seems fact, and one stands on the threshold of that secret lotus land of purple glooms one knew as a child.

LILIAS RIDER HAGGARD

The Green Children

∻

Clac straightened his back, braced his aching shoulders, and grunted. Sweat trickled down his face and dripped from the end of his nose. He licked his lips; they tasted of salt. Clac glanced down the long, straight swaths of corn; then, rubbing the back of his neck between his shoulder blades, he considered the position of the sun. But his stomach was his best clock. He filled his lungs, cupped a huge hand to his mouth, and bellowed 'FOOD'.

The other cottars heard him. One by one they stopped work and mopped their brows; one by one they left their own strips of land and began to walk slowly towards him.

Their scythes gleamed in the midday sun; a very small wind moved over the swathes and whispered warnings to the ears of uncut corn.

'Come on,' called Clac. He sat on the turf balk dividing his strip from the next, waiting impatiently. 'This sun . . . I've had enough of it.'

'So have I,' sighed Swein, collapsing in a heap like a sack of potatoes.

'Come on,' cried Clac. 'You and you and all the rest of you.' He picked up a flitch with one hand and with the other a gourd of cider. 'I'm for the shade. Shade first, then food. Who'll carry the apples?'

'I will,' said Grim.

So the cottars, nine of them in all, set off across the common land, on which their cattle grazed. They walked towards the wolfpits – where, in winter, wild creatures roamed – and towards the high, waving elms.

✥

Clac led the way. He always did; he liked leading. And the lord of the manor, Sir Richard de Calne, who had recognised this quality in him, had put him over the other cottars and villeins. As the tired, hungry men approached the elms, Clac stopped in his tracks. 'Look!'

'What?' said Grim.

'Where?' said Swein.

'Look!' Clac exclaimed again. 'Look! There!' He pointed towards the trees. 'Follow me.' And throwing down the flitch and the gourd, he started to run. He ran and ran until at last he came to the old wolfpits just beyond the elms.

'Look!' insisted Clac, pointing again. 'Look!'

And there, huddling in the hollow of the largest pit, the cottars saw what Clac had seen: two green children. Their skin was green, their hair was green, they wore green clothes. And one was a boy, the other was a girl.

For a moment, nobody moved, nobody spoke. The cottars looked down at the green children and the green children looked up at the cottars.

'Blessed Edmund preserve us!' exclaimed Clac. And he made the sign of the cross.

'And St William of Norwich,' muttered Grim. And he crossed himself too.

'Who can they be?' said Swein helplessly.

'Ask them,' said Clac.

Swein laughed nervously.

'All right then,' said Clac. 'I will. I'll ask them.'

The cottars bunched together anxiously.

'They might be little folk,' Swein warned him.

'Let's leave them alone,' said Thurketil.

'Look at them,' Clac replied. 'Do they look as if they mean harm?'

The cottars crowded round the edge of the pit, watching breathlessly. If one man had moved, the rest would have toppled headlong down. The boy and the girl were clutching one another, looking up at the nine men fearfully. And then the green girl buried her face in her hands and began to sob.

'You see?' said Clac. He stepped forward, slipped down the grassy bank, and walked towards the children.

The closer he drew, the more astonished he became – so much so that he completely forgot his nervousness. In all his thirty years, he had never seen or even heard of anything like it before: green fingers, and, poking out of their green sandals, green toes.

'Hello!' said Clac in his gruff, friendly voice. 'Who are you?' And he smiled encouragingly.

The children huddled still closer together. They gazed at Clac, bewildered, and said nothing.

Clac looked at the children closely and guessed the girl was about nine and the boy about seven. He saw that they resembled each other not only because they were green, but also in the mould of their features. 'You must be brother and sister,' he said. 'Who are you? Where do you come from?'

The children continued to gaze at him silently.

'Well,' thought Clac. 'It's clear enough: either they're dumb or they don't understand me.'

At this moment the boy turned to the girl and spoke several strange words.

'That settles it,' said Clac. 'You don't understand me. And I can't pretend to understand you.'

The green girl looked at Clac; suddenly, she flashed a smile at him, opened her mouth and pointed at it.

'Blessed Edmund preserve me!' exclaimed Clac. 'She's got a green tongue.' He nodded and grinned. 'I see,' he said. 'You're hungry.'

He turned round, waved reassuringly to the other cottars, and called, 'What are you doing up there, you idlers? Get the flitch and bring it down. And bring the cider too.'

In no time, the cottars were pouring down into the pit, bringing the food with them. They swarmed round the children, their superstition at last overcome by curiosity.

'Here! Give me the flitch,' said Clac.

Swein passed it to him.

Clac sniffed at it, then showed it to the two children.

They looked at it blankly, then turned to each other and shook their heads. Then the girl sniffed it, and wrinkled up her nose.

'Look at that!' marvelled Clac. 'They've never seen a flitch before.'

Now it was his turn to shake his head. 'What about the apples, then?' he said. 'Give me two red apples.'

'Here,' said Grim, and passed them over.

The two children looked at them, turned to each other again, and shook their heads a second time.

Clac was dumbfounded. He didn't know what to do but he didn't like to admit it. 'How about that?' he asked. 'How about that? They've never seen apples before.'

Despite their behaviour, it was clear that the two children were famished. Again and again they pointed to their mouths. And once more the green girl began to weep.

'I think we should take them to Sir Richard,' said Clac. The other cottars nodded in agreement.

'Sir Richard's a traveller,' Clac continued. 'He's travelled far and wide, almost as far as the edges of the earth. Perhaps he's heard of green children.'

So the cottars escorted the green children to the manor of Sir Richard de Calne. And as they walked, they sang, for they were not altogether sorry to miss an afternoon's work under the blazing sun. But the children were dazzled by the bright light. They kept their heads down, and shielded their eyes with their arms.

The fortified manor was surrounded by a moat. Clac strode to the brink, and shouted to the guards on the other side. For a while the guards conferred, then they let the drawbridge down. The little group, with the children in their midst, walked across and on into the great hall.

'Wait here!' said a guard, his eyes bulging out of his head as he looked at the two children. 'Until Sir Richard comes.'

Inside the hall, out of the sunlight, the children looked about them with great curiosity. They ran to and fro, exclaiming in wonder at the huge stone fireplace, the narrow window-slits, the yellow rushes on the floor. They chattered excitedly, and for a moment even forgot their hunger.

❖

'Green children,' boomed a voice at the entrance of the hall. 'What's all this?'

The cottars swung round.

And there, hands on hips, stood Sir Richard de Calne, an enormous, pot-bellied man.

The cottars liked him well. He was just a lord, and a generous one, though his moods were as variable as the weather: one day he was laughing and smiling, the next thundering commands to his frightened servants.

But now he was completely silent. He was staring at the green children open-mouthed.

'Please my lord,' said Clac, stepping forward. And he explained to Sir Richard how he had discovered the green children at the wolfpits. 'And they don't speak English,' he said, 'and they won't eat our food.'

From his great height, Sir Richard looked down at the shrinking children. He frowned and stroked his beard.

Sir Richard liked problems; he enjoyed solving them. But green children, green as grass, who couldn't speak English, who wouldn't eat apples . . . that was another thing altogether.

'So they don't speak English,' echoed Sir Richard after a long pause. 'Ah well! I don't blame them. Perhaps they speak Norman.' He stooped, smiled warmly at the green girl, and began, 'D'ou venez-vous?'

The green girl gazed at him blankly. Then she looked to her brother; he shrugged his shoulders, and repeated the strange words that Clac had heard in the wolfpits. Whereupon the girl looked up at Sir Richard, pointed at his pot-belly and opened her mouth.

Sir Richard bellowed with laughter. 'I understand you,' he cried. 'Food's a common language. All right. Sit them down.' Then walking to the entrance of the hall, he shouted at the top of his voice, 'FOOD! FOOD!'

Clac led the two children over to the trestle table and sat them at the wooden bench. In no time, a servant bustled in, bearing part of a chicken on a platter; a second followed, carrying a bunch of succulent, black grapes; and the third brought a pitcher of red wine. 'Give them each a wing,' said

Sir Richard. 'That'll tempt them. You see if it doesn't.'

But the children pushed the chicken away, indicating that they would not eat it.

'What about the grapes, then?' suggested Sir Richard.

The black, succulent grapes were set before them. The girl fingered one and said something to her brother. Then they refused them too.

Sir Richard strode up and down the hall, disconcerted. 'Bring them some cheese, then,' he instructed.

A servant hurried out of the hall, reappeared with a bowl of cream cheese, and placed it on the table. The two children took one look at it and pushed that away too.

'Well!' exclaimed Sir Richard. 'I don't know. What *will* they eat?'

At this moment, it so happened that an old servant was crossing the far end of the hall. In his arms, he carried a pile of freshly cut beans, still attached to their stalks.

Seeing the beans, the green children cried out with delight. They leaped up from the bench and ran toward the old man who was so startled at the sight of them that he threw down the beans on the spot and ran out of the hall as fast as his old legs could carry him.

The children fell upon the pile and immediately began to tear open the stalks, thinking the beans were in the hollows of them. Finding none, they were utterly dismayed and began to weep dismally once more.

'Look!' said Clac. 'Like this.' He quickly opened a pod and showed them the naked beans.

And so at last the green children began to eat.

The cottars stood watching them.

'I see' said Richard eventually. 'I see. Green children, green food.'

After they had eaten their fill, the green children smiled gratefully at Sir Richard de Calne and the cottars.

'Well! Now what?' said Sir Richard. 'What are we going to do with them now?'

This was a question no one could answer. And as the two children showed no inclination to leave the hall, Sir Richard instructed that they should be allowed to remain at the manor for as long as they desired. He asked his priest, Father John, to teach them to speak English.

And for many, many months the green children ate nothing but beans.

✜

The great fair at Stourbridge came and went. Sir Richard de Calne journeyed there, laden with packs of wool, and returned with Baltic furs, French cloth and lace, and salts and spices from the East. And all this time the green children stayed at the manor. Father John took his duties seriously; each day the children had English lessons with him. They both worked hard and made good progress.

And the old priest, a lean, angular man who often declared he loved no one but God, began to love the green boy and the green girl as if they were his own children.

'They must be baptised,' he told Sir Richard one day. 'They may be green but they still have souls.'

And so the children were baptised. The ceremony was attended by Sir Richard de Calne and by all his household, and by his cottars and villeins.

August grew old; September was born. High winds wrestled with the sun. Leaves fell, carpeting the earth in copper and bronze and gold. The elms by the wolfpits looked like skeletons.

Clac and his fellow cottars brought the harvest home and began to prepare for winter. They killed pigs and cattle and fowls, and gave them to their wives who cut them up, and salted them, and stored them away for harder days.

During the cold days of November, the green boy became listless. He would eat no more beans; he made little progress in his work; he lost interest in playing draughts and spinning tops; and nothing his sister said could cheer him.

Nobody could say what was wrong with him; he ran no fever, sported no spots. And his sister could speak so little English she was unable to explain.

Father John was anxious. He made the green boy eat mugwort and mayweed, crab-apple, thyme and fennel; he sent to Bury for water from the Well of Our Lady; he offered prayers.

It was all to no avail. One dark day, when the ground was like iron underfoot and the shifting skies were grey, the green boy threw up his hands and died.

Throughout the long hard winter his sister could not be consoled. Often she wept; it was so cold the tears froze on her cheeks. But at last, as spring threw off winter, she too threw off her grief. The crocuses flowered.

One evening Sir Richard de Calne and his family, his servants and guards, and all the cottars and villeins who worked on his demesne, gathered in the great hall.

First the company ate. The food was drawn from earth and air and sea. There was crane and swan, peacock and snipe; there was sucking-pig and, out of season, venison; there were lampreys, sea-trout and sturgeon. And to wash down this sumptuous fare, there was spiced wine.

After the meal it was customary for the minstrel to sing. The company turned from the tables to face the minstrel and the fire.

'Not tonight,' called Sir Richard. 'We'll not have songs tonight. I've asked you all for a special reason.' He paused and looked round the all. 'Our guests,' he continued, and smiling turned to the green girl, 'can speak English at last. She has told me who she is, and where she comes from. And now I have asked her to tell her story to you.'

There was a rustle of excitement.

The green girl stood up and walked over to the minstrel's place beside the flickering fire. Her shadow danced on the wall behind her. All at once she smiled, the same alluring smile she had first flashed at Clac in the wolfpits. Then she began in a strong, clear voice, 'I come from a green country. The people are green, the animals are green, the earth and sky are green. There is nothing that is not green.

'The sun never shines in my country. The light there is a constant green glow, as if the sun was always just below the horizon.'

A puff of woodsmoke filled the room. The listeners coughed and rubbed their smarting eyes, then settled again. They had never heard such a thing in their lives.

'From the hills of our country,' said the girl, 'you can see another, much brighter land – though I have never been there – divided from ours by a broad river.'

'But tell us where your land is,' said Sir Richard, 'and how you got here.'

'Well! One day my brother and I . . . my poor brother who died of homesickness . . . we were tending sheep on the hills, and they began to stray. We followed them and came to the mouth of a cave, a great cave we'd never seen before. The sheep entered the cave and we walked in after them. And there, ahead of us, we heard the sound of bells: a most beautiful sound, loud bells and soft bells, treble bells and bass bells, ringing, ringing.

'It seemed,' said the green girl, 'that the sound came from the far end of the cave. The bells were so beautiful they pulled us towards them. We *had* to find them. So we walked through the cave, on and on. At first it was flat; then we began to climb. And the bells rang and rang, tugging us towards them.

'The cave was gloomy but not dark; then, suddenly, we saw a bright light some way ahead of us. "That's where the bells are coming from," my brother said. So we hurried towards it. It grew and grew, dazzling us. And all at once we climbed up and out, out of the cave,' said the girl. 'The ringing stopped, the sunlight blinded us.' She clapped her hands to her eyes. 'We were knocked senseless by the sun. We lay in a swoon for a long time . . .'

Everyone in the hall was leaning forward. The fire roared.

'When we recovered our senses, we saw we were in some deep pit. And although we looked for the entrance to the cave, it had completely gone; we couldn't find it again. "What shall we do?" my brother asked me. "I don't know," I said. I felt rather afraid. "But as we can't go back, we'd better go forward." So, very cautiously, we climbed out of the wolf-pits . . .'

'That's it,' exclaimed Clac excitedly. 'I remember. That's when I saw you.'

The green girl smiled.

'"Blessed Edmund preserve me!" I said,' continued Clac. 'Two green children!'

'If you were surprised to see green children,' the girl replied, 'think how astonished we were to see pink men!'

Everyone laughed. 'Not only astonished,' continued the green girl, 'but frightened too. My brother and I backed down into the pit again. But we couldn't find the entrance to the cave; and so you caught us.'

The assembled company sighed, and nodded their heads.

'That's my story,' said the green girl. 'The rest you know. Thank you all for your great kindness to me. I've been very happy here; but if ever I can find the entrance to the cave, I must return home.'

With that, she sat down.

But that was only the beginning. Many were the questions asked of her that night; many were the answers given.

But the years passed and the green girl did not return

home. She remained at the manor, for she was unable to find the entrance to the cave.

In time she learned to eat meat, and the fruits of the earth, and even to enjoy them. And slowly her skin lost its green tinge, her hair became fair.

She always said that she was very happy in this world. But often Clac and the cottars saw her wandering down by the wolfpits, alone. At such times, they never went near her. For they knew that she must be lonely for her own people, and looking for the entrance to the cave.

One spring the green girl married. She left the manor of Sir Richard de Calne and went to live with her husband near the port of Lynn. But even then she used to return to the wolfpits from time to time. Her feet were anchored to this earth, but her heart and mind sailed on to another far-off land.

✣

How, then, did it end? What became of the girl who climbed up from the green land? All this happened years and years ago. Eight hundred years ago. Some things live longer than centuries, others do not. We know much about the green girl, but there is much we do not know.

And nobody knows – unless you do – whether the green girl lived on earth to the end of her days; or whether, one day, near the wolfpits, she simply disappeared.

Oh Dunwich is beautiful. I am on
a heaving moor of heather and close
gorse up and down and ending in a
sandy cliff about 80 feet perpendicular
and the black, peat-strewn fine sand
below. On the edge of this 1½ miles
away is the ruined church that has half
fallen over already. Four arches and a
broken tower, pale and airy. Just
beyond that the higher moor dips to
quite flat marsh with gentlest rises
inland with masses of trees compact
and dark and a perfect huge curve of
foamy coast up to the red light at

Southwold northward. In the other direction, just behind us, the moor dips to more marshes with black cattle dim and far off under white sun, and three faint windmills that work a sluice and then trees – inland more gentle rises with pines.

EDWARD THOMAS

Sea Tongue

✢

I am the bell. I'm the tongue of the bell. I was cast before your grandmother was a girl. Before your grandmother's grandmother. So long ago.

Listen now! I'm like to last. I'm gold and green, cast in bronze, I weigh two tons. Up here, in the belfry of this closed church, I'm surrounded by sounds. Mouthfuls of air. Words ring me.

High on this crumbling cliff, I can see the fields of spring and summer corn; they're green and gold, as I am. I can see the shining water, silver and black, and the far fisherman on it. And look! Here comes the bellringer – the old bellwoman.

✧

I am the bellwoman. For as long as I live I'll ring this old bell for those who will listen.

Not the church people: they have all gone. Not the seabirds; not the lugworms; not the inside-out crabs nor the shining mackerel. Whenever storms shatter the glass or fogs take me by the throat, I ring for the sailor and the fisherman. I warn them off the quicksands and away from the crumbling cliff. I ring and save them from the sea-god.

✧

I am the sea-god. My body is dark; it's so bright you can scarcely look at me, so deep you cannot fathom me.

My clothing is salt-fret raised by the four winds, twisting shreds of mist, shining gloom. And fog, fog, proofed and damp and cold. I'll wrap them around the fisherman. I'll wreck his boat.

I remember the days when I ruled earth. I ruled her all – every grain and granule – and I'll rule her again. I'll gnaw at this crumbling cliff tonight. I'll undermine the church and its graveyard. I'll chew on the bones of the dead.

✧

We are the dead. We died in bed, we died on the sword, we fell out of the sky, we swallowed the ocean.

To come to this: this green graveyard with its rows of narrow beds. Each of us separate and all of us one.

We lived in time and we're still wrapped in sound and movement – gull-glide, gull-swoop. We live time out, long bundles of bone bedded in the cliff.

✧

I am the cliff. Keep away from me. I'm jumpy and shrinking, unsure of myself. I may let you down badly.

Layers and bands, boulders and gravel and grit and little shining stones: these are earth's bones. But the sea-god keeps laughing and crying and digging and tugging. I scarcely know where I am and I know time is ending. Fences. Red flags. Keep away from me. I'm not fit for the living.

✧

We are the living. One night half of a cottage – Peter's cottage – bucketed down into the boiling water and he was left standing on the cliff-edge in his night-shirt.

After that, everyone wanted to move inland. We had no choice. You've only to look at the cracks. To listen to the sea-god's hollow voice!

Every year he comes closer. Gordon's cottage went down. And Martha's. And Ellen's. The back of the village became the front. And now what's left? Only the bellwoman's cottage, and the empty shell of the church.

✧

I am the church. I remember the days when the bellows wheezed for the organ to play. I remember when people got down on their knees and prayed.

I've weathered such storms. Winds tearing at the walls, flint-and-brick, salt winds howling.

And now, tonight, this storm. So fierce, old earth herself is shaking and shuddering. Ah! Here comes the old bellwoman.

✧

I am the bellwoman. There! Those lights, stuttering and bouncing. There's a boat out there, and maybe ten.

Up, up these saucer steps as fast as I can. Up!

Here in this mouldy room, I'll ring and ring and ring, and set heaven itself singing, until my palms are raw. I'll drown the sea-god.

✜

I am the sea-god. And I keep clapping my luminous hands.

Come this way, fisherman, over the seal's bath and here along the cockle-path. Here are the slick quicksands, and they will have you.

Fisherman, come this way over the gulls' road and the herring-haunt! Here, up against this crumbling cliff. Give me your boat.

✜

I am the boat. To keep afloat; to go where my master tells me: I've always obeyed the two commandments.

Now my master says forward but the sea-god says back; my master says anchor but the night-storm says drag. My deck is a tangle of lines and nets and ropes; my old heart's heavy with sluicing dark water. I'm drowning; I'm torn apart.

Groan and creak: I quiver; I weep salt. Shouts of the fishermen. Laughter of the sea-god. Scream of the night-storm.

✜

I am the night-storm. I AM THE STORM.

Down with the bell and down with the belfry. Down on the white head of the bellwoman. Down with the whole church and the tilting graveyard. Down with the cliff itself, cracking and opening and sliding and collapsing. Down with them all into the foam-and-snarl of the sea.

I'm the night-storm and there will be no morning.

✜

I am the morning. I am good morning.

My hands are white as white doves, and healing. Let me lay them on this purple fever. Let them settle on the boat.

Nothing lasts for ever. Let me give you back your eyes, fisherman.

✤

I am the fisherman. I heard the bell last night. Joe and Grimus and Pug, yes we all did! I heard the bell and dropped anchor. But there is no bell. There's no church, there's no belfry along this coast. Where am I? Am I dreaming?

Well! God blessed this old boat and our haul of shiners. He saw fit to spare us sinners. We'll take our bearings, now, and head for home.

But I heard the bell. And now! I can hear it! Down, down under the boat's keel. I can hear the bell.

✤

I am the bell. I am the tongue of the bell, gold and green, far under the swinging water.

I ring and ring, in fog and storm, to save boats from the quicksands and the rocky shore. I'm like to last; I'm cast in bronze, I weigh two tons.

Listen now! Can you hear me? Can you hear the changes of the sea?

Sweet Suffolk Owl, so trimly dight
With feathers, like a lady bright,
Thou sing'st alone, sitting at night
Te whit! Te whoo! Te whit! Te whit!

Thy note that forth so freely rolls
With shrill command the mouse controls,
And sings a dirge for dying souls –
Te whit! Te whoo! Te whit! Te whit!

THOMAS VAUTOR

The Spectre of Wandlebury

✛

Sir Osbert Fitzhugh and his squire rode down the spine of England. They rode south from the Border over the moors, under the peaks, into the heart, around the fens, and at last they reached Cambridge Castle.

'I'm in search of wonders,' Sir Osbert told his ancient host, as they sat at the fire.

'All around us,' the old man said, 'and all too many. Boggarts and bogles, and dead hands in the fen, woodwoses and phantoms . . .'

'Tell me more,' said Osbert, and his bushy brown eyebrows twitched.

'And the nearest wonder is the greatest.'

Osbert's squire glanced over his shoulder, and to his eyes the whole gloomy hall looked alive in the firelight with memories and dancing shadows.

'Wandlebury,' said the host. 'Haven't you heard of it?' The fire crackled and spat.

'There's an old earth-fort near here. Wandlebury. People say that if you enter it alone under the full moon, and shout "Knight to knight! Show yourself!". . .'

'What then?' asked Osbert.

'Then a knight will appear out of the darkness. Out of air! A spectre! He's mounted and fully armed and ferocious. He'll joust with his challenger and hurl him to the ground.'

'And if the challenger throws the spectre?' asked the squire.

The ancient host looked at the eager young squire. 'That has never happened,' he said.

For a while the three of them sat in silence in front of the licking, sucking, swallowing, biting, spitting fire.

'Alone,' said the old man again. 'You have to go in to the earth-fort alone. Through the three ramparts. Your squire can wait and watch outside.'

'Full moon,' said Osbert thoughtfully, and then he vigorously rubbed both his eyebrows. 'All right! I'll challenge him.'

'You will?' cried the host.

'Who risks nothing wins nothing,' said Osbert.

'They say the old gods are buried up there,' the old man said. 'Up there on the hillside where earth and sky meet.'

✢

The moon was clean and acute; the stars were like sky-gorse.

Sir Osbert and his squire clattered over the moat and rode away to the south-east. First they followed an old track, then they galloped out onto the Gogmagog Hills, and the ramparts of Wandlebury reared up in front of them.

Just in front of the entrance – a gap in the earth-wall – the two riders reined in.

'Remember our host's warning?' Osbert said. 'Alone! And you must wait here.'

The squire nodded.

Osbert stared at the hill-fort and then he put his right hand on the squire's shoulder. He seemed to be on the very point of saying something but perhaps he thought better of it, for abruptly he dug in his heels, broke into a canter, and entered the fort.

It was very still inside the waiting ramparts. Watchful and chill and almost airless.

Osbert looked about him. Then slowly he rode right round the inside of the fort, and the moon's face shone so brightly he could see every molehill.

When Osbert had completed the circuit, he drew up, pulled off his gauntlets and put his mouth to his knuckles and fists and blew on them.

'All right!' he said in a low voice. And then much louder: 'All right!'

Sir Osbert Fitzhugh walked his horse to the centre of the fort. There he raised his lance and shook it at the moon, and then he shouted out, 'Knight to knight! Show yourself!'

First there came a whinny and a snort. And then, out of the darkness, out of air, as if he were made of them, there rode a knight – a knight or whatever he was. He rode right up to Sir Osbert.

Under the steely light of the moon, Osbert looked at him: his sombre armour and death-dark shield, his superb jet-black mount with its charcoal trappings. Osbert looked and he knew that, behind his closed visor, the Knight of Wandlebury was looking at him.

'Will you fight?' he asked, and he licked his lips. 'Will you joust?'

By way of reply, the figure couched his lance and rode away to the far side of the fort. Osbert couched his lance, too, and walked his nervous horse in the opposite direction. Then both knights wheeled round and at once galloped back towards each other.

Their armour clinked and rang; their leather straps and saddles creaked and groaned; the hooves of their mounts pounded, pounded on the ground.

But try as he would, Osbert was unable to balance his lance; and when the two knights met, its gleaming tip was still pointing at Orion, the shining hunter. The Knight of Wandlebury's aim was fearsome, though. His lance grazed Osbert's left cheek-guard – within an inch of staving in his visor or crushing his windpipe.

When they tilted at each other for a second time, neither knight was able to hit the other, and their two horses careered away into the darkness. But at the third end, Osbert was the more skilful. He drove his lance against his opponent's breast-bone, just under the heart, and the dark knight was thrown right over his horse's crupper.

At once, Osbert galloped after the riderless black horse. Round and round the inside of the earth-fort he chased it, until he was able to grab its bridle.

'I claim him!' roared Osbert. 'I claim him!'

The Knight of Wandlebury slowly got on to his hands and knees; he got to his feet. He began to stagger towards Osbert and then, fully armed as he was, he broke into a kind of run.

Osbert saw he had drawn a short spear and, still grasping the black horse's bridle, he laid his right hand on his sword hilt. It was of no use, though. He hadn't even unsheathed it before the dark knight raised his flashing spear and flung it at Osbert.

Osbert felt a savage stab of pain just under his right hip. He screwed up his eyes. And when he opened his eyes again, the dark knight had vanished. Into the darkness. Into air.

Still mounted, Sir Osbert slowly led the magnificent horse out of the earth-fort and, at the entrance, his squire was waiting for him.

'Where did he go?' gasped Osbert. 'Which way?'

'He vanished, sire,' said the squire. 'In the winking of an eye. He vanished.'

'On foot!' said Osbert, with some satisfaction.

'Are you hurt, sire?' asked the squire.

'It's nothing,' said Osbert. 'Warm water. Wine.'

'You are hurt,' said the squire, and gently he took the bridle of the black horse from his lord's left hand. 'Let me lead him back to the Castle.'

Sir Osbert Fitzhugh and his squire rode down off the Gogmagog Hills. They followed the old track north and west and, a few minutes before cockcrow, they clattered over the moat into the courtyard of Cambridge Castle.

There they tethered the black horse and their own mounts. Then the squire put one hand under Sir Osbert's right shoulder, and helped him up the lamplit steps into the great hall.

To their surprise, their ancient host was still sitting in his great oak chair beside the fire. He had waited up for them through the watches of the night and, when he heard their footsteps, he roused himself, rubbed his eyelids and stretched. His face was pink and scrubbed, and as unlined as a baby's.

'You fought with him,' the old man said. 'You fought with the spectre.'

Sir Osbert Fitzhugh inclined his head, and then he staggered sideways.

'Sire,' said the squire. 'He is hurt.'

'Sit here, man,' said the host, guiding Osbert to his own seat by the fire.

Then the squire unlaced the greave covering Osbert's right

leg, and when he took off his metal boot, he saw the blood swilling around in it.

'Never mind that!' said Osbert. 'Water! Wine! You must see the black horse.'

'The black horse!' exclaimed the old man.

'The Knight of Wandlebury's horse,' said the squire.

'Everyone must see this wonder,' said the host. 'Wait here! Let me wake my servants.'

✛

Sir Osbert and his squire and their ancient host led the way down to the courtyard, and a tumble of grumbling, groaning servants followed them. They were all wearing nightshirts and were wrapped in woollen blankets, hempen sacks, animal skins – anything to keep out the dawn-cold.

Then the grumbling and groaning stopped. Everyone marvelled at the magnificent black horse. One of the grooms reckoned he was at least eighteen hands high. In the first light, more grey than green, more green than blue, they could all see that his glossy coat and mane and tail were raven black. And they saw the look in his rolling eyes – fierce and almost wild.

But then the cock crew, and the moment it did so, the black horse reared up on its tether, and its eyes rolled terribly. It snorted and whinnied and stamped. Sparks danced around its hooves. Then it reared up again, right over the watching crowd, and snapped its tether.

At once the black horse galloped out of the castle courtyard. The ancient host tottered after it, and the squire and many of the servants ran after it, but no – they couldn't catch up with it. They couldn't even see it. It had vanished into the vanishing night.

✛

In the castle, wise women applied salves and poultices to Sir Osbert's thigh-wound. Days passed, like cloud-shadows racing over the fields, and at last the knight and his squire took leave of their ancient host. They rode north, around the fen, into the heart, under the peaks, over the moors. They rode up the spine of England and at last they reached the Border.

But every year, for as long as he lived, on the same night he had jousted with the spectre, Sir Osbert's thigh-wound burst open. It oozed, it bled and filled his right shoe with blood.

Pal Hall was once leading a cart drawn by a donkey up Castle Hill. The cart contained a ladder. Half way up, Pal said to himself, 'It seems to be hard going for the donkey. If I carry the ladder myself, it will ease it a lot.' So he got into the cart and put the ladder on his shoulder.

Pal Hall once built a waggon in his workshop. He made a good job of it but, when he had finished, found that it was too big to go through the door, and he had to take it to pieces before he could get it out.

A neighbour was showing Pal Hall his runner beans which were just appearing above the ground. Pal saw the kernels, which had been pushed up to the surface, and said, 'They're coming up upside down. Take 'em all out, and plant them the right way up.'

ANONYMOUS

A Pitcher of Brains

⁘

Near here and not so long ago either, there lived a fool. And he was such a fool that he was always getting into trouble, and being laughed at by everyone. So he decided to buy a pitcher of brains.

'You can get everything you want from the wise woman who lives on the hilltop,' people told him. 'She deals in potions and herbs and spells and things, and can tell you everything that will happen to you or your family.'

So the fool went to his mother and asked her whether he should go to the wise woman and buy a pitcher of brains.

'That you should!' she said. 'You need them badly enough. And if I were to die, my son, who would take care of a poor fool like you? You're no more fit to look after yourself than a

newborn baby.' The fool's mother wagged her forefinger. 'Mind your manners, and speak to her nicely, my lad. The wise people are easily put out.'

So off went the fool after his tea, and there was the wise woman, sitting by the fire, and stirring a big pot.

'Good evening, missus,' he says. 'It's a fine evening.'

'Yes,' says she, and she went on stirring.

'Maybe it'll rain,' he says, and he stood first on one foot and then on the other.

'Maybe,' says she.

'And maybe it won't,' he says, and looked out of the window.

'Maybe not,' says she.

And the fool scratched his head, and twisted round his hat.

'Well!' says the fool, 'I can't think of anything else to say about the weather, but let me see: the crops are getting on fine.'

'Fine,' says she.

'And . . . and . . . the beasts are fattening,' he says.

'They are,' says she.

'And . . . and . . .' he says, and he came to a stop. 'I reckon we'll get down to business now; we've done the polite bit. Have you got any brains for sale?'

'That depends,' says she. 'If you want king's brains, or soldier's brains, or schoolmaster's brains, I don't keep them.'

'Heavens, no!' he says. 'Just ordinary brains fit for any fool – the same as everyone else around here. Just something common-like.'

'Yes, then,' says the wise woman. 'I might manage that, if you're ready to help yourself.'

'How can I do that, missus?' he says.

'Like this,' says she, peering into her pot. 'You bring me the heart of the thing you like best, and I'll tell you where to get your pitcher of brains.'

'But,' says the fool, scratching his head, 'how can I do that?'

'That's not for me to say,' the wise woman says. 'Find out for yourself, my lad, unless you want to be a fool all your days. But you'll have to answer me a riddle so I can be sure you've brought me the right thing, and have got your brains about you. And now,' says the wise woman, 'I've something else to see to – so good day to you!' And she carried the pot away with her into the back room.

So off went the fool to his mother, and he told her what the wise woman had said.

'And I reckon I'll have to kill that pig,' he says, 'for I like bacon fat more than anything.'

'Then do it, my lad!' says his mother. 'It will certainly be a marvellous thing if you're able to buy a pitcher of brains, and look after yourself.'

So the fool killed the pig; and next day off he went to the wise woman's cottage, and there she sat, reading a great book.

'Good day, missus!' he says. 'I've brought you the heart of the thing I like best of all. I'll put it on the table here – it's wrapped in paper.'

'Oh, yes?' says she, and she looked at him through her spectacles. 'Tell me this, then: what runs without feet?'

The fool scratched his head, and thought, and thought, but he couldn't say.

'Go away!' says she. 'You haven't found me the right thing yet. I've no brains for you today.' And she banged the book shut, and turned her back.

Off went the fool to tell his mother. But when he got near the house, people came running out to tell him his mother was dying. And when he got in, his mother simply looked at him, and smiled, as if to say she could leave him with a quiet mind, since he'd got brains enough now to look after himself – and then she died.

So the fool sat down, and the more he thought about it, the

worse he felt. He remembered how she'd nursed him when he was a little baby, and helped him with his lessons, and cooked his dinners, and mended his shoes, and put up with his foolishness, and he felt sorrier and sorrier, and began to sigh and sob.

'Oh, mother, mother!' he says. 'Who'll take care of me now? You shouldn't have left me alone, for I liked you better than anything!'

As soon as he said that, the fool thought of the wise woman's words. 'Hi, yi!' he says. 'Have I got to cut out my mother's heart and take it to the wise woman? I don't like this job.' And he took out a knife and tested its edge.

'No, I can't do it,' says the fool. 'What shall I do to get that pitcher of brains now I'm alone in the world?' So he thought and thought and then he went and borrowed a sack; he bundled his mother into it, and carried it on his shoulder up to the wise woman's cottage.

'Good day, missus!' he says. 'I reckon I've found you the right thing this time, and that's for sure.' And he plumped the sack down – kerflap! – on the doorstep.

'Maybe,' says the wise woman. 'But now tell me this: what's yellow and shining but isn't gold?'

The fool scratched his head, and thought, and thought, but he couldn't say.

'Well! You haven't hit on the right thing, my lad,' says she. 'I do believe you're a bigger fool than I thought!' And she shut the door in his face.

'Look at me, then,' says the fool, and he sat down by the roadside and sobbed. 'I've lost the only two things I cared for, and what else can I find to buy a pitcher of brains with?' And with that, the fool fairly howled, until the tears ran down into his mouth.

Then up came a girl who lived nearby, and she looked at him. 'What's up with you, fool?' says she.

'Oo! I've killed my pig, and lost my mother, and I'm nothing but a fool myself,' he says between sobs.

'That's bad,' she says. 'And haven't you got anybody to look after you?'

'No,' he says, 'and I can't buy my pitcher of brains because there's nothing left that I like best!'

'What are you talking about?' says she.

Then down she sat, next to the fool, and the fool told her all about the wise woman and the pig, and his mother and the riddles, and said he was alone in the world.

'Well!' says she, 'I wouldn't mind looking after you myself.'

'Could you manage?' he says.

'Oh, yes!' says she. 'People say fools make good husbands, and I reckon I'll have you, if you're willing.'

'Can you cook?' he says.

'Yes, I can,' says she.

'And scrub?' he says.

'To be sure!' says she.

'And mend my shoes?' he says.

'I certainly can,' says she.

'Then I reckon you'll do as well as anybody,' the fool says. 'But what shall I do about this wise woman?'

'Oh, wait a bit!' says she. 'Something may turn up. It doesn't matter whether you're a fool or not, so long as you've got me to look after you.'

'That's true,' he says. So off they went and got married.

The girl kept his house so clean and neat, and cooked him such tasty dinners, that one night the fool said to her, 'Lass, I've been thinking I like you better than anything, when all's said and done.'

'That's good to hear,' says she. 'And so?'

'Have I got to kill you and take your heart up to the wise woman for the pitcher of brains?'

'Lord, no!' says the girl, looking scared. 'I wouldn't do that.

But see here: you didn't cut out your mother's heart, did you?'

'No,' says the fool. 'But if I had, maybe I'd have got my pitcher of brains.'

'Not a bit of it,' says she. 'Just you take me up as I am, heart and all, and I bet I can help you answer the riddles.'

'Can you really?' the fool says, doubtfully.

'Well,' says she, 'let's see now. Tell me the first one.'

'What runs without feet?' he says.

'Why, water!' says she.

'It does,' says the fool, and he scratched his head. 'And what's yellow and shining, but isn't gold?'

'Why, the sun!' says she.

'Faith, it is!' the fool says. 'Come! Let's go to the wise woman at once!' So off they went and, as they walked up the path, they saw her sitting at her door, twining straws.

'Good day, missus,' the fool says.

'Good day, fool,' says she.

'I reckon I've found you the right thing at last,' he says. 'But I haven't cut the heart out. It's such mucky work.'

The wise woman looked at them both, and wiped her spectacles. 'Can you tell me what has no legs at first, and then two legs, and ends up with four legs?'

The fool scratched his head, and thought, and thought, but he couldn't say.

Then the girl whispered in his ear: 'It's a tadpole.'

'Maybe,' says the fool, 'it might be a tadpole, missus.'

The wise woman nodded her head. 'That's right,' says she, 'and you've got your pitcher of brains already.'

'Where are they?' the fool says, looking around, and feeling in his pockets.

'In your wife's head,' says she. 'The only cure for a fool is a good wife to look after him, and that you've got so good day to you!' And with that she nodded to them, and stood up and went into her house.

So the fool and the girl went home together, and the fool never wanted to buy a pitcher of brains again. His wife had enough for them both.

Not a sound broke the silence as I waited there
by the edge of a pool which gleamed like silver in the
moonlight. One by one the lights from the distant
village faded and presently the shouts and laughter
of the merrymakers at Wells died away on the breeze.
Then there settled down a grim stillness which seemed
pregnant with menace and I clasped my stick the
tighter as I realized my absolute loneliness . . .

After what seemed a long interval, a gentle sighing
came from away by the seashore, some two or three
miles off, and the moonlight grew steadily brighter.
Then, as I watched from the cover of my hollow, I saw
an indefinable shadow, far away on the horizon. The
eerie silence was rent by the most appalling howl to
which I have ever listened – it froze the blood in my
veins and caused my hair to stand right on end. And
the shadow was coming nearer. Believe me or not, as
you will, it may have all been imagination or the result
of the tales I had previously heard; but I saw that black
hound as clearly as I shall ever see anything again . . .

With a yell of terror I jumped from the hollow and fled. Not once did I look behind, but I felt that the creature was in pursuit. Never had I run as I ran that night. Stumbling, cursing, breathing heavily, I tore up the lane and at last gained the threshold of the cottage. With a profound feeling of thankfulness I knocked upon the door and called to the cottager to open. In a moment a light appeared above and footsteps descended and came along the passage. Then I heard a welcome voice – 'Do yew not be jiffling, sir, I be a-coming.'

And as the bolt was undone and the key turned I glanced around to see a pair of ferocious eyes fixed upon me and to feel on my neck a scorching breath. The hound was actually about to spring as the door opened and I fell fainting into the arms of my host. One look he gave and then shut the door with a bang as a great black body seemed to leap through the air, and come thudding on the ground outside . . .

On the following morning I told the full story and heard only the comment, 'Yew be a durned fool and lucky to escape at that.'

CHRISTOPHER MARLOWE

The Black Dog
of Bungay

✣

'That's a queer old morning,' said the man.

'That's been a queer summer,' his wife replied.

True, it hadn't rained on St Swithin's Day. And true, the hay harvest was laid in, no worse than most years and better than some. But as everyone agreed, it was impossible to say what the weather would be like from one day to the next.

'Hear that?' said the man.

His wife stopped and listened.

'The redshank's warning,' said the man.

As the couple made their way to church on the first Sunday after Lammas, the cornfield swayed and beat around them

like an angry gleaming ocean. Nine o'clock on a August morning and it was half-dark in the village of Bungay, caught in a noose of the river, fifteen miles from Norwich and fifteen miles from the sea.

'Coming in?' shouted the man to the church warden who was perched up on the roof, cleaning the gutter.

Whatever the warden replied was swept away on the tides of air. The man and his wife couldn't hear a word.

'Old heathen!' the woman said.

Inside the church, it was even darker. In the gloom, the pale faces in their pews shone like anemones. And the wind, wrestling and tugging at the old walls, unable to force its way in, made the stillness in that place seem all the greater – something greater than the gathering storm and yet something you could almost reach out to and touch.

The man and his wife and all the villagers, gathered to hear divine service and common prayer, listened to the stillness, and the mounting wind, and the tolling bell.

'Let us pray,' said the priest.

There was a flash of lightning then. Every window in the church flickered and danced and for a moment the aisle shone brilliantly with a freezing light. The thunder followed before the man and his wife had time even to look at each other: a fearful crack, then a deep-throated, long-drawn roll. After that came the rain, tapping and rapping so that the whole roof over their heads seemed to be one throbbing pulse.

'Let us pray,' called the priest.

Inside the church, it was dark now. The priest could not see his congregation, the man and his wife could not even see beyond their own noses.

'The corn,' muttered the man. 'It'll flatten the corn.'

'What have we done?' said his wife, clutching her husband's arm. 'What wrong have we done?'

Such was the fury of the storm that no one in that building was not afraid for his life.

Then the lightning struck again. Men and women screamed and thought they had come to the end of the world. In the dazzling light, a huge black dog leaped out from the altar and raced down the length of the church. The church quaked and staggered, and the kneeling villagers dived to left and right, burying their heads in their arms. And so they remained, crying and clutching, heaped in scrums higgledy-piggledy, while the thunder smashed into their skulls and roared inside them.

When the man opened his eyes, he saw that the worst of the darkness was passing; the light in the church was like the first light of dawn. He clambered to his feet, and then peered at the old man motionless in the pew in front of him.

'Look!' he heard himself say.

The old man was still kneeling, as if in prayer – and it was exactly the same with the old woman in the pew opposite. But the heads of them both were lolling sideways. Their eyes were open and their necks were broken; both were stone dead.

Then the man and his wife were caught up in the commotion behind them. People were gathering around a young lad. Two of them gently lifted him and laid him face down on a pew.

'As the dog raced down the aisle,' said the priest, 'it sprang at him. With one claw, it gouged his back.'

The lad was unconscious because of the pain. Then the church door swung open. Everyone turned and jumped. It was the church warden. 'The thunder,' he said. 'It threw me off the roof.'

'The dog,' said the voices out of the gloom. 'That was the dog.'

'My elbows!' said the warden. 'My shoulders!'

'What an escape!' said the man.

'My knees!' said the warden.

'You old heathen!' said the woman.

As the villagers stepped out of the church, they saw the black dog had savaged the church door and porch with his claws. Neither human flesh nor solid oak nor blocks of limestone had been able to withstand him.

And, once they were outside, they saw the face of the church clock had turned black, and lost its hands. The warden climbed up to it and looked out and shouted down, 'The wires! The wheels! They're all twisted and torn and broken into pieces.'

The villagers of Bungay looked after the lad with the gouged back. They dressed his deep wound, and bandaged it, and plied him with meat and drink. But although he survived, his working days were done. As the wound closed up, he shrank and shrivelled like a piece of leather, scorched by hot fire, or like the mouth of a purse or a bag, drawn together by string.

News of the black dog spread far and wide. And for as long as the young lad lived, people came to Bungay to see him and to talk to him. Long after he had died, they came to see the church clock. And when that was mended, they came, as they still come, to see the claw marks on the door and in the porch.

'That's not the first time men have seen the black dog,' said the man.

'No,' said his wife. 'And that won't be the last.'

There was a fat lady from Eye
Who felt she was likely to die;
    But for fear that once dead
    She would not be well-fed
She gulped down a pig,
    a cow,
    a sheep,
        twelve buns,
        a seven-layer cake,
            four cups of coffee,
            and a green apple pie.

That's None of Your Business

✛

That clock! It was like a piece of icing done by a goddess, dropped out of heaven.

It was white as white, and inlaid with little mirrors and misty pearls. The tick-and-tock of it were as close and comforting as the beats of your own heart, and the music it made on the hour, each hour, seemed to come straight from paradise.

Every boy and girl in the village came round to listen to it, and look at it. How longingly they looked at it!

So when they grew up and I grew old, and had little time for grand possessions, I thought I just might give it away. I said I'd give it to whoever could mind his own business – or

her own business, for that matter – for a whole year.

At the end of the year, a year all but a few minutes, there was a knock on the door. A young man had come to ask for the clock.

'I've minded my own business for a whole year,' he said.

I believed him. He was a dull sort of lad, the kind that never asks questions and doesn't seem too interested in other people or the wonders of the world.

As I went into the next room to fetch the clock, I called out, 'You're the second young man, you know, who's come to claim the clock.'

'The second!' exclaimed the young man. 'Why didn't the first one get it?'

'That's none of your business,' I said. 'And *you* won't get the clock.'

So I left the clock on the mantelpiece. There it is! Inlaid with little mirrors and misty pearls. It's like a piece of icing done by a goddess, dropped out of heaven.

I took notice of a strange decay of the sex
here (the Essex marshes) insomuch that it is
very frequent to meet with men that had from
five or six to fourteen or fifteen wives, nay, and
some more . . . The reason as a merry fellow
told me was this: that they, being bred in the
marshes themselves and seasoned to the
place, did pretty well, but that they always
went up into the uplands for a wife. That
when they took the young lasses out of the
wholesome, fresh air they were healthy, but
they presently changed complexion, got an
ague or two, and seldom held it above half a
year, or a year at most. 'And then,' said he,
'we go to the uplands again and fetch another.'
So that marrying of wives was reckoned a
kind of farm to them.

DANIEL DEFOE

The Strangers' Share

✣

Have you heard about the Strangers? Who? The Strangers.

There used to be heaps of them around; yes, and there still are. Do I really believe in them? Have I seen one? Yes, that I have. I've seen them often. I saw one only last spring.

The marshmen and marshwomen mainly call them the Strangers or else Little People, because they're no bigger than newborn babies. Or else they call them Greencoaties, because they wear green jackets; or sometimes the Earthkin, because they live in the earth. But mainly the Strangers, because that's what they are: strange in their looks and habits, strange in their likes and dislikes, and strangers amongst the marsh people.

They're very little creatures, no more a span from top to

toe, with arms and legs as thin as thread, but great big feet and hands, and heads rolling around on their shoulders.

They wear grass-green jackets and breeches, and have yellow bonnets on their heads, for all the world like toadstools. Their faces are strange, with long noses, and wide mouths, and great red tongues hanging out and flap-flapping about.

I've never heard one talk, I don't think. But when they're upset about anything, they grin and yelp like angry hounds, and when they feel merry and cuddlesome, they twitter and cheep as softly and sweetly as the little birds.

When I was a boy, and my grandfather was a boy, the Strangers showed themselves more often than now, and people weren't as afraid of them as you'd have thought. If they were crossed, they were mischievous angry things; but provided they were left alone, they didn't harm anyone or meddle with anybody's business. And if people were good to them, they never forgot it, and would do anything to help them out in return.

On summer nights, they danced in the moonlight on the great flat stones you see lying around here. I don't know where the stones came from, but my grandfather told me his grandfather told him that, long ago, the marsh people used to light fires on the stones, and smear them with blood, and thought a lot more about the Strangers than about the parson and the church.

And on winter nights, when people were in bed, the Strangers would dance in the hearth; and the crickets played for them for all they were worth.

Yes, the Strangers were always in the thick of things. At harvest time, they pulled at the ears of corn, and tumbled amongst the stubble, and wrestled with the poppy-heads. And in the year's spring, they were busy shaking and pinching the leaf-buds and blossom-buds on the trees, to open them, and tweaking the buds of flowers, and chasing the butterflies, and tugging the worms out of the earth. They were always playing around like tomfools, but they were happy and no worse than mischievous so long as they weren't crossed. You had only to stay mum, and keep still as death, and you'd see the busy little things running and playing all round you.

The marsh people knew the Strangers helped the corn to ripen, and all the green things to grow; and knew they painted the pretty colours of the flowers, and the reds and browns of the fruit in autumn, and the yellowing leaves. Then they thought how, if the Strangers got upset, all the green things would dwindle and wither, and the harvest would fail, and everyone would go hungry. So they did everything they could think of to please the little people, and to stay friends with them.

In each garden, the first flowers and the first fruit, and the first cabbage or whatever, would be taken to the nearest flat stone, and laid on it for the Strangers. In the fields, the first ears of corn, or the first potatoes, were given to the little people. And in each home, before people sat to eat, a bit of bread and a drop of milk or beer was spilled into the fireplace, in case the Greencoaties were hungry or thirsty.

But as time went by, the marsh people grew sort of careless. Maybe they went more to church and thought less about the Strangers, and the customs of their fathers; maybe they forgot the old tales their grandfathers had told them; or maybe they thought they'd grown so wise that they knew better than all the generations before them.

Anyhow, and however it happened, the flat stones of the Strangers stayed bare; the first fruits of the earth were withheld, and people sat to their food without sparing a crumb for the fireplace. The little people were left to look after themselves, and to hunger and thirst if that's what they wanted.

I reckon the Strangers couldn't make it out at first. I don't know, maybe they talked it over amongst themselves. For a long time, though, they kept quiet and never showed they were upset with the marsh people's unfriendly ways. Perhaps to begin with they just couldn't believe people would grow so careless about the Earthkin – after all, they'd been good neighbours to the marshmen and marshwomen for longer than I can tell. But as time went on, they couldn't help but see the truth of it, for people got worse and worse every day. Yes, and they took the very stones of the Strangers from the fields and the sides of lanes, and threw them away.

So it went on, and the marsh children grew up to be men and women, and scarcely knew a thing about the little people who had been such friends of their parents and grandparents. And the old folk had almost completely forgotten about them.

But the Strangers hadn't forgotten – no! they remembered the earlier times only too well, they did, and they were only waiting for a good chance to pay back the marsh people for their bad manners. And at last it came. It was slow to come just as the marsh people were slow to forget their regard for the little people; but it was sure – it was sure as hell-fire.

Summer after summer the harvest failed, and the green things dwindled, and the animals fell sick. Summer after summer the crops came to nothing, and the marsh fever got worse, and children sickened and died, and whatever the marsh people put their hands to went wrong and arsy-versy.

Summer after summer things were like this, until the marsh people lost heart, and instead of working in the fields they sat on their doorsteps, or by their fires, waiting for better luck to come their way. But better luck never came near them – not a glimpse of it! Food became scarce, children moaned for hunger, and babies wasted away.

And when the fathers looked at their wives, with their dead babies at their breasts, and turned their hollowed eyes from their sickly children who moaned for bread, what could they do but drink until they were merry, and their troubles forgotten until next day? In time, some of the women consoled themselves in the same way, while others took to stuffing themselves stupid with opium, whenever they could get hold of it, and the children died all the faster. Everything was so terrible that people thought it was the Day of Judgement, and the beginning of hell itself.

But one day the wise women met together; and they did the dreadful things they never talk about, and with fire and blood they discovered the truth of it. Then they tramped through the little marsh hamlets and into the yards, and into the inns, and up and down the whole shire, and they called on the marsh people to meet them next evening as soon as it grew dark. And the people wondered and scratched their heads, but the next night they all came to the meeting-place by the crossroads to listen to the wise women.

Then the wise women told them everything they'd found out.

'The Strangers are working against us, and meddling with everything,' said one wise woman. 'They're meddling with our crops and our animals, and with our babies and children. Our only chance is to make it up with the little people.'

'Our parents and our grandparents and the generations before them used to keep friendly with the Strangers,' said another wise woman. 'They gave them the first fruits of the field and the first fruits of the garden. They gave them food. But in the end they stopped all that kind of thing, and pretty well turned their backs on the Greencoaties.'

'The little people have been very patient,' said the third wise woman. 'They've waited, and waited for a long time, to see if we'd return to the old ways. But at last the time came to pay us all back, and so trouble and bad times have come to the marsh, as you all know.'

'I call on every man who has seen his animals starving,' said the first wise woman, 'and on every man who has seen some job going arsy-versy.'

'I call on every woman,' said the second, 'who has heard her children sob for bread, and had none to give them, and has buried her poor little baby before it was even out of her arms.'

'Do as your parents and grandparents used to do,' said the third wise woman. 'Tell the old stories, listen to the old stories, make friends again with the little people! Get this curse lifted from you!'

Before long, the marshmen were shaking hands on the wise women's words, and the women were sobbing as they thought of their dead babies and hungry children – and they all went home to do their best to put the wrong right.

Well! I can't tell you everything, but as the curse of the Strangers had come, so it went: slowly, slowly, the bad luck got better. The little people were upset, and the old times weren't to be won back in one day or even one summer. But first fruits were laid on the flat stones wherever the stones could be found; and bread and drink were spilled on the hearth, as they used to be, and the old people told the children all the old stories, and taught them to believe them, and to give time and thought to the bogles and boggarts and the green-coated Strangers.

And slowly, slowly, the little people stopped being angry. They got on with the marsh people again, and lifted the curse they had laid upon them. And slowly, slowly, the harvest got better, and the animals got fatter, and the children held up their heads; but for all that, it wasn't the same as it used to be.

The marsh men took to gin and the women to their opium; they were always shaken by fevers, and the children were yellow and puny. Times were better, and people did well enough, and the Strangers weren't at all unfriendly, but things were still not as gay as in the times when the marsh people hadn't known what it was to go hungry and thirsty, before the evil days when the churchyard was so full with the little graves, and cradles in people's homes sometimes rocked dead children.

Ah! And all this came of turning from the old ways. I reckon it's best to keep to them, in case bad luck should be sent as payment for bad manners.

The dandelion is used as a plant of omen by young men and maidens. When its seeds are ripened, they stand above the head of the plant in a globular form, with a feathery tuft at the end of each seed, and then are easily detached. The flower stalk must be plucked carefully, so as not to injure the globe of seeds, and you are then to blow off the seeds with your breath. So many puffs as are required to blow every seed clean off, so many years it will be before you are married.

Another plant of omen is the yarrow, called by us yarroway. The mode of divination is this: you must take one of the serrated leaves of the plant, and with it tickle the inside of the nostrils, repeating at the same time the following lines:

> *Yarroway, yarroway, bear a white blow;*
> *If my love love me, my nose will bleed now.*

If the blood follows this charm, success in courtship is held to be certain. If a brake is cut across, the veins are supposed to show the initials of the name of the future husband.

JOHN GLYDE

Cape of Rushes

✤

There was once a very rich gentleman, and he had three daughters. He thought he'd see how fond of him they were, so he says to the first, 'How much do you love me, my dear?'

'Why,' says she, 'I love you as much as I love my own life.'

'That's good,' he says. So he asks his second daughter, 'How much do you love me, my dear?'

'Why,' says she, 'more than all the world.'

'That's good,' he says. So he asks his third daughter, 'How much do *you* love me, my dear?'

'Why,' says she, 'I love you as much as fresh meat loves salt.'

The man was very angry. 'You don't love me at all,' he says, 'and there's no room for you in this house.' So he drove her out there and then, and shut the door in her face.

The third daughter turned away, and she walked and walked until she came to a fen. And there she gathered a lot of rushes, and made them into a cape – a kind of cloak with a hood – to cover her from head to foot, and to hide her fine clothes. And then she walked on and on, until she came to a great house.

'Do you want a maid?' she says.

'No, we don't,' they say.

'I've nowhere to go,' she says, 'and I'd ask no wages, and do any sort of work.'

'Well,' they say, 'if you want to wash the pots and scrape the saucepans, you can stay.'

So there she stayed, and washed the pots and scraped the saucepans, and did all the dirty work. And because she never told them her name, they called her Cape of Rushes.

One day there was to be a grand dance a little way away, and the servants were given time off to go and look at the fine people. Cape of Rushes said she was too tired to go, so she stayed at home.

But when the servants had gone, she threw off her cape of rushes, and cleaned herself up, and went to the dance. And no one there was so finely dressed as she.

Well, who should be there but her master's son? And what did he do but fall in love with her the minute he set eyes on her? He wouldn't dance with anyone else.

But before the dance was over, Cape of Rushes stepped off the floor, and away she went home. And when the other maids came back, she pretended to be asleep with her cape of rushes on.

Next morning, they said to her: 'You did miss a sight, Cape of Rushes!'

'What was that?' says she.

'Why, the most beautiful lady you ever saw, marvellously dressed. The young master, he never took his eyes off her.'

'I should have liked to see her,' said Cape of Rushes.

'Well,' they say, 'there's to be another dance this evening, and perhaps she'll be there.'

But, come the evening, Cape of Rushes said she was too tired to go with them. When the servants had gone, though, she threw off her cape of rushes, and cleaned herself up, and away she went to the dance.

The master's son had been counting on seeing her. He danced with no one else, and never took his eyes off her.

But before the dance was over, she slipped away and home she went; and when the maids came back, she pretended to be asleep with her cape of rushes on.

Next day they said to her again: 'Cape of Rushes, you should have been there to see the lady. She was there again, looking marvellous, and the young master, he never took his eyes off her.'

'Well, there,' she says, 'I should have liked to see her.'

'Well,' says they, 'there's a dance again this evening, and you must come with us, for she's sure to be there.'

When evening came, Cape of Rushes said she was too tired to go, and say what they would, she stayed at home. But when the servants had gone, she threw off her cape of rushes, and cleaned herself up, and away she went to the dance.

The master's son was delighted when he saw her. He danced with no one but her, and never took his eyes off her. When she wouldn't tell him her name, or where she came from, he gave her a ring, and told her that if he didn't see her again he would die.

Well, before the dance was over, away she slipped, and home she went; and when the maids came home she was pretending to be asleep with her cape of rushes on.

Next day they said to her: 'There, Cape of Rushes, you didn't come last night, and now you won't see the lady, for there are to be no more dances.'

'I'd very much have liked to see her,' she says.

The master's son, he tried every way to find out where the lady had gone, but turn where he would, and ask whom he might, he couldn't find out a thing. He became more and more ill because of his love for her, until he had to keep to his bed.

'Make some soup for the young master,' they told the cook. 'He's dying for love of the lady.' And the cook was just about to begin when Cape of Rushes walked in.

'What are you doing there?' she says.

'I'm going to make some soup for the young master,' says the cook, 'because he's dying for love of the lady.'

'Let me make it,' says Cape of Rushes.

Well, the cook wouldn't let her at first, but at last she said yes; and Cape of Rushes made the soup. And when she had made it, she slipped the ring into it on the sly, before the cook took it upstairs.

The young man drank it, and saw the ring at the bottom.

'Send for the cook,' he says. So the cook comes up.

'Who made this here soup?' he says.

The cook was frightened. 'I did,' she says.

But then the young master looked at her. 'No, you didn't,' he says. 'Tell me who made it, and you'll come to no harm.'

'Well, then, it was Cape of Rushes,' says she.

So Cape of Rushes was called up.

'Did you make the soup?' he says.

'Yes, I did,' says she.

'Where did you get this ring?' he says.

'From him who gave it to me,' says she.

'Who are you, then?' says the young man.

'I'll show you,' says she. And she threw off her cape of rushes, and there she was in her beautiful clothes.

Well, the master's son very soon got better, and he and Cape of Rushes were to be married not long after. It was to be a very grand wedding, and everyone was invited, from near and far. And Cape of Rushes' father was asked, but Cape of Rushes never told anyone who she really was.

Before the wedding she went to the cook, and she said, 'I want you to prepare all the dishes without a grain of salt.'

'They'll taste horrible,' said the cook.

'That doesn't matter,' she says.

'Very well,' says the cook.

Well, the wedding day came, and Cape of Rushes and the young man were married. And after the marriage, all the guests sat down to the wedding breakfast.

When they tried the meat, it was so tasteless they just couldn't eat it. Cape of Rushes' father tried first one dish and then another, and then he burst into tears.

'What's the matter?' asked the master's son.

'Oh!' says he, 'I had a daughter. And I asked her how much she loved me. And she said, 'As much as fresh meat loves salt.' I shut the door in her face because I thought she didn't love me. But now I see she loved me best of all. And she may be dead for all I know.'

'No, father, here she is,' says Cape of Rushes.

And she goes up to him and puts her arms round him. And so they were happy ever after.

Cutting your nails on Monday
means health;
Tuesday, wealth;
Wednesday, news;
Thursday, new shoes:
Friday, sorrow;
Saturday, seeing your sweetheart
the next day;
Sunday, the devil.

TRADITIONAL

Samuel's Ghost

✤

Poor little Samuel! He was asleep when his cottage caught fire, and when he woke up it was too late. He was only a lad and he was burned to death; he got turned into ashes, and maybe cinders.

After a while, though, Samuel got up. The inside of him got up and gave itself a shake. He must have felt rather queer: he wasn't used to doing without a body, and he didn't know what to do next, and all around him there were boggarts and bogles and chancy things, and he was a bit scared.

Before long, Samuel heard a voice. 'You must go to the graveyard,' said whatever it was, 'and tell the Big Worm you're dead.'

'Must I?' said Samuel.

'And ask him to have you eaten up,' said the something.

'Otherwise you'll never rest in the earth.'

'I'm willing,' said Samuel.

So Samuel set off for the graveyard, asking the way, and rubbing shoulders with all the horrid things that glowered around him.

By and by, Samuel came to an empty dark space. Glimmering lights were crossing and recrossing it. It smelt earthy, as strong as the soil in spring, and here and there it gave off a ghastly stink, sickening and scary. Underfoot were creeping things, and all round were crawling, fluttering things, and the air was hot and tacky.

On the far side of this space was a horrid great worm, coiled up on a flat stone, and its slimy head was nodding and swinging from side to side, as if it were sniffing out its dinner.

Samuel was afraid when he heard something call out his name, and the worm shot its horrid head right into his face. 'Samuel! Is that you, Samuel? So you're dead and buried, and food for the worms, are you?'

'I am,' said Samuel.

'Well!' said the worm. 'Where's your body?'

'Please, your worship,' said Samuel – he didn't want to anger the worm, naturally 'I'm all here!'

'No,' said the worm. 'How do you think we can eat you? You must fetch your corpse if you want to rest in the earth.'

'But where is it?' said Samuel, scratching his head. 'My corpse?'

'Where is it buried?' said the worm.

'It isn't buried,' said Samuel. 'That's just it. It's ashes. I got burned up.'

'Ha!' said the worm. 'That's bad. That's very bad. You'll not taste too good.'

Samuel didn't know what to say.

'Don't fret,' said the worm. 'Go and fetch the ashes. Bring them here and we'll do all we can.'

So Samuel went back to his burned-out cottage. He looked and looked. He scooped up all the ashes he could find into a sack, and took them off to the great worm.

Samuel opened the sack, and the worm crawled down off the flat stone. It sniffed the ashes and turned them over and over.

'Samuel,' said the worm after a while. 'Something's missing. You're not all here, Samuel. Where's the rest of you? You'll have to find the rest.'

'I've brought all I could find,' said Samuel.

'No,' the worm said. 'There's an arm missing.'

'Ah!' said Samuel. 'That's right! I lost an arm I had.'

'Lost?' asked the worm.

'It was cut off,' said Samuel.

'You must find it, Samuel.'

Samuel frowned. 'I don't know where the doctor put it,' he said. 'I can go and see.'

So Samuel hurried off again. He hunted high and low, and after a while he found his arm.

Samuel went straight back to the worm. 'Here's the arm,' he said.

The worm slid off its flat stone and turned the arm over.

'No, Samuel,' said the worm. 'There's something still missing. Did you lose anything else?'

'Let's see,' said Samuel. 'Let's see . . . I lost a nail once, and that never grew again.'

'That's it, I reckon!' said the worm. 'You've got to find it, Samuel!'

'I don't think I'll ever find that, master,' said Samuel. 'Not one nail. I'll give it a try, though.'

So Samuel hurried off for the third time. But a nail is just as hard to find as it's easy to lose. Although Samuel searched and searched, he couldn't find anything; so at last he went back to the worm.

'I've searched and searched and I've found nothing,' said Samuel. 'You must take me without my nail – it's no great loss, is it? Can't you make do without it?'

'No,' said the worm. 'I can't. And if you can't find it – are you quite certain you can't, Samuel?'

'Certain, worse luck!'

'Then you must walk! You must walk by day and walk by night. I'm very sorry for you, Samuel, but you'll have plenty of company!'

Then all the creeping things and crawling things swarmed round Samuel and turned him out. And unless he has found it, Samuel has been walking and hunting for his nail from that day to this.

Some countyes vaunte themselves in pyes,
And some in meat excelle;
For turnippes of enormous size
Fair Norfolk bears the belle . . .

At midnight houre a hardie knighte
   Was pricking o'er the ley
The starres and moone had loste their light
   And he had loste his waye . . .

Now voices straunge assaile his eare,
   And yet ne house was nie:
Thoughte he, the Devil himself is here,
   Preserve me God on hie!

Then summon'd hee his courage hie,
    And thus aloud 'gan call;
Fays, gyauntes, demons, come not nie,
    For I defye you all!

When from a hollow turnippe neare
    Out jumped a living wighte;
With friendly voice, and accent cleare,
    He thus address'd the knighte.

Sir knighte, ne demon dwelleth here
    Ne gyaunte keepes his house
But tway poor drovers, goodman Vere,
    And honest Robin rouse.

We tweyne have taken shelter here,
    With oxen ninety-two;
And if you'll enter, nivir feare,
There's room enough for you.

ANONYMOUS

Tom Hickathrift

✦

Before the reign of William the Conqueror, there lived in the marshes of the Isle of Ely a man whose name was Thomas Hickathrift. He was a poor man, a labourer, but very strong and able to do two days' work in one. He called his one son by his own name, Thomas, and sent him to a good school. But Tom was none too clever; indeed, he was a bit soft in the head, and would not apply himself, so he learned nothing.

When Thomas Hickathrift died, Tom's mother went out to work. She loved her son dearly, and supported him as best she could. But Tom himself was so slothful that he would not turn his hand at anything, let alone do a good day's work. He liked nothing so much as to loaf in the chimney corner, and ate as much at one sitting as would four or five normal men.

When he was only ten years old, Tom was eight foot tall; he measured sixty inches round the waist and his hand was like a shoulder of mutton. There was no part of him that was not outsize.

One day, Tom's poor mother went to ask her neighbour, a rich farmer, if he could spare her a bundle of straw.

'Take as much as you want,' said the farmer, who was an honest, charitable man.

Tom's mother hurried home and said to her son, 'Will you go up to the farm and fetch me a bundle of straw?'

'Let me be!' said Tom.

'No,' said Tom's old mother. 'Please go.'

'I'll only go,' said Tom, 'if you can borrow a cart rope for me.'

Tom's mother needed the straw, and saw she would not get it without humouring her son. So she went off to another neighbour and borrowed a cart rope.

Then Tom got out of the chimney corner, took the rope, and walked up to the farm. He found the farmer in the barn, watching two farmhands thresh the corn. 'My mother has told me to come up for a bundle of straw,' he said.

'Take as much as you can carry, Tom,' said the farmer.

Tom stretched out the rope on the barn floor, and laid the straw along it – armful after armful.

'If you go on like that,' said one farmhand, 'your rope will be too short to go round it.'

The farmer and the other lad shook their heads at Tom's stupidity, but Tom took no notice. He gathered more straw, and then drew the rope round it all.

'You won't be able to carry that,' said one lad.

'It'll weigh a whole ton,' said the farmer. 'Twenty hundred-weight.'

'What a fool!' jeered the other.

By way of answer, Tom lifted the bundle and swung it on to

his shoulder. He made no more of it than if it had weighed a single hundredweight and, turning his back on the farmer and his two lads, strode out of the barn.

When Tom's strength became known, his neighbours gave him no rest. Nobody would let him go on basking by the fire and everybody wanted to hire him to do this job and that job. Seeing how strong he was, they told him it was a disgrace that he should lead such a lazy life, and do nothing from day to day.

Tom became so tired of this baiting and taunting that he set to work, disposing of one job after another. Then, one day, a man came to Tom's house and asked him to help bring back a tree trunk from a nearby wood.

Tom agreed, and the man hired four other lads besides. When they reached the fallen tree in the wood, the man and the lads placed the cart alongside it and tried to hoist it with pulleys. But they were unable to move the tree one inch.

'Stand back, you fools!' said Tom. He bent down, and lifted the trunk so that it stood on one end. Then he laid it on the cart.

'There!' said Tom. 'There's a man's work for you.'

'It is and all,' said the man, marvelling.

Just as they were coming out of the wood, Tom and his companions met the forester and exchanged greetings. 'Can you spare a stick,' asked Tom, 'for my old mother's fire?'

'Of course,' said the forester. 'Take whatever you can carry.'

Tom looked around and saw another fallen tree, even larger than the one lying in the cart. He humped it on to one shoulder, and then he walked home with it as fast as six horses could have drawn it on the cart.

When Tom realised that he had more strength than twenty men, he began to enjoy himself. For the first time in his life, he made good friends with other lads. He ran races against them, and held jumping contests and, delighting in their company, went with them to fairs and meetings to see the sports and other amusements.

Tom once went to a fair that had attracted every lad in the district – some went to cudgel, some to wrestle, some to throw the hammer. For a time Tom stood and watched this sport and that sport, and then he approached a group of young men who were throwing the hammer.

'Here's a manly sport,' said Tom.

'It is,' said the young men. 'Do you want to try your hand?'

Tom took the hammer in one hand and tried it for weight. 'Stand out of the way then,' said Tom.

'Yes, yes,' said the blacksmith.

'Stand out of the way!' said Tom. 'I'm going to throw it as far as I can.'

'Yes, yes, Tom,' jeered the blacksmith, winking at his friends. 'I'm sure you'll be able to throw it a great distance.'

Tom grasped the hammer and threw it. It soared through the air and fell smack into a river more than a thousand yards off.

'Yes,' said Tom to the blacksmith, and he smiled. 'Now you can go and fetch your hammer.'

After Tom had shown his strength at throwing the hammer, he thought he would try his hand at wrestling. He had no more skill than an ass, and all that he did, he did by brute force. Yet he threw each young man who stood against him – they were done for as soon as Tom took a grip on them. Some opponents he threw over his head, some he spread-eagled at his feet. He never engaged in clinches and never tripped anyone; he simply picked them up and hurled them two or three yards, so that they were in danger of breaking their necks. Before long, there was nobody left who was ready to climb into the ring with Tom. They all took him to be some devil come amongst them; and Tom's fame spread more widely than ever.

Tom took such delight in sport that he would travel near or far to any fair or festival that promised cudgel-play or bear-baiting or a game of football. So when he was out riding one day in a part of the country where he was a stranger, and happened to come across a group of lads who were playing football for a wager, Tom dismounted at once and watched the game for a while.

One of the players mis-kicked the ball and it bounced towards Tom. Tom swung a leg and gave the ball such a boot that the players saw it fly through the air, and no one could tell how far it had gone and where it had come to ground. They were unable to find their ball again and their game was ruined.

First the players were astonished, then they rounded on Tom and called him a wrecker.

Tom said nothing. He walked across to a nearby house that had collapsed in a recent storm, picked up a beam, and began to lay about him. All those who got in the way he either killed or stunned. The whole district was up in arms against Tom, but they were helpless; no one was able to stand up to him.

It was quite late that evening before Tom made his way home. On the road, he met four thieves notorious for robbing people who passed that way. No one could escape them, and they robbed everyone they came across, both rich and poor.

When they saw Tom, alone as he was, they thought he would be easy prey, and they would soon have their money. They were mistaken; it was the other way round!

'Stand and deliver!' shouted the thieves.

'What?' said Tom. 'What should I deliver?'

'Your money, sir,' they said.

'My money,' said Tom. 'First you must ask for it better; and second, you must be better armed.'

'Come,' said the men. 'We're not here to gossip. We're here

for your money, and your money we'll have before you move from this place.'

'Really?' said Tom. 'Well, then, you must come and get it.'

One of the thieves thrust at Tom but Tom grabbed his sword, which was made of trusty steel, and struck so fiercely at the others that they were afraid for their lives, and spurred their horses. Tom was not having that. Seeing one of the thieves was carrying a portmanteau behind him, and rightly taking it to be stuffed with money, Tom redoubled his efforts. He killed two of the thieves and wounded the other two so grievously that they begged for mercy. Tom spared their lives but took all their money – two hundred pounds in all – to sweeten his journey home.

The next day, when Tom was walking through the forest near his home, he met a brawny tinker who had a good strong staff over one shoulder and a large dog who was carrying his bag and tools.

'Where are you from?' asked Tom. 'And where are you going? There's no highway here.'

'Mind your own business,' said the tinker. 'Only fools are meddlers.'

'Mind my own business!' roared Tom. 'Mind my own business!' And with that, he put his fist in front of the tinker's nose.

'All right,' said the tinker. 'It's three long years now since I had a scrap. I've challenged countless men but nobody dares fight me. As far as I can see, this whole county is full of cowards.' The tinker grinned. 'Though I have heard,' he added, 'that there's a strong lad hereabouts called Tom Hickathrift. I'd like to meet him, all right. I'd like to have a turn with him.'

'Yes,' said Tom, 'and he might well get the better of you. Here he is. You've met him.'

'What?' said the tinker.

'I am he,' said Tom. 'Now what do you say?'

'Why,' cried the tinker, 'I'm delighted that we've met, if only by accident. Now we can try our strength on each other.'

'All right!' said Tom. 'Let me get a twig first.'

'Of course,' said the tinker. 'Hang the man who fights an unarmed man! I've got no time for that.'

So Tom stepped over to the nearby gate and wrenched off the diagonal bar for a staff. Then they started fighting; the tinker thrust at Tom and Tom thrust at the tinker. They fought with the strength of two giants. The tinker was wearing a leather coat and every time Tom struck him the coat screeched, but for all that the tinker didn't give Tom an inch.

But then Tom gave the tinker a blow on the side of his head that felled him. 'Now, tinker!' said Tom. 'Now where are you?'

But the tinker was nimble. He leaped up again and struck Tom with his staff so that Tom staggered sideways; the tinker rained blow after blow on Tom, and then swiped at his head from the other side so that Tom's neck cracked with the strain.

Tom threw down his weapon. 'You're a match for me, tinker, and more than a match,' he said. 'Come home with me now!' So he took the tinker home to recover from his wounds and bruises, and from that day onward, they were the best of friends.

✧

Tom's fame spread far and wide, and came to the ears of a brewer in King's Lynn who needed a good strong man to carry his beer across the marshes to Wisbech.

Tom was not eager to work for him, but the brewer begged him, and offered him a new suit of clothes from top to toe, and as much good food and drink as he desired. So Tom at last agreed to work for the brewer, and the brewer told him exactly which way to go. For there was a monstrous giant who ranged over part of the marsh, and nobody dared go near him. Those who did, he either killed or used as his servants.

Tom did more work in one day than all the other men employed by the brewer did in three. The brewer was delighted, and made Tom his chief assistant; every day Tom carried the beer to Wisbech and a long way it was – twenty miles along the road that skirted the marsh and twenty miles back again.

Tom found the journey wearisome and he knew that the quickest way to Wisbech, over the land where the giant lived, would be less than half the distance. Eating so well and drinking so much strong ale day after day, Tom was half as powerful again as he had been before; and so, one morning, without saying anything to the brewer or his fellow servants, he decided he would either get to Wisbech by the quicker route or lose his life – win the horse, as people say, or lose the saddle.

Tom drove his horses and cart and flung open the gates of the marsh path. It wasn't long before the giant spied Tom and stormed up to him, intending to seize all his beer as a prize. He greeted Tom like a lion. 'Who gave you the right to come this way?' he roared. 'Haven't you heard that everyone is afraid of the sight of me? How dare you fling open the gates to my land just as you please?'

Tom stood there and said nothing. He didn't give a fart for the giant.

'Have you no thought for your life?' asked the giant. 'I'll make an example of you for all the other rogues under the sun. You see how many heads are hanging on that tree over there, the heads of men who have trespassed against me? Your head will hang higher than the rest.'

'A turd in your teeth!' said Tom. 'You won't find I'm quite the same as them.'

'You're nothing but a fool,' said the giant. 'What do you think you're doing, coming here to fight me? You haven't even got a weapon.'

'I have a weapon here,' said Tom, 'that will show you up for a rogue and a coward.'

'Right!' said the giant, and he ran into his earth-cave to fetch his great club, meaning to dash out Tom's brains with the first blow.

Now Tom didn't know what to do for a weapon, for he could see his whip would be little use against the giant who was twelve foot tall and six foot round the waist. But while the giant was getting his club, he had a good idea. He over-turned his cart, and grasped one wheel and the axletree for shield and buckler.

The giant came out of his cave and stared at Tom, amazed to see him holding the wheel in one hand and the axletree in the other. 'You're going to do a great job with those weapons,' he bawled. 'I've got a twig here that will beat you and your wheel and axletree into the ground.' The giant's twig was as thick as a mill post but Tom was not afraid. He saw there was nothing for it but to kill or be killed.

Then the giant struck at Tom with his club. Tom parried the blow with his shield and the rim of the wheel cracked. But Tom, meanwhile, struck at the giant with his axletree. He hit him on the side of his head and made him reel. 'What?' said Tom, 'Are you drunk on my strong beer already?'

The giant recovered and rained blows on Tom. But Tom parried them all with his wheel so that he was not hurt at all. And he in turn struck such savage blows that sweat and blood streamed down the giant's face. Being fat and foggy and almost exhausted by the long fight, the giant asked Tom, 'Let me drink a little. Then we'll fight again.'

'No, no,' said Tom. 'I never learned enough from my mother to be such a fool.' Tom saw the giant was beginning to weary, and felt his blows were becoming weaker, and thought it was best to make hay while the sun shone. So he assaulted the giant with one blow after another until at last he felled him.

The giant roared and bawled and begged Tom not to kill him. He offered to do anything for Tom, even to be his servant. But Tom had no more mercy on him than on a wild bear. He went on hitting him until he was dead and then he cut off the giant's head.

Then Tom went into the giant's cave and looked around. He found such a store of gold and silver that his heart leaped at the sight of it. After a while, however, he left it all as it was and calmly continued his journey to Wisbech, where he delivered the beer just as usual.

When Tom got home, he told his master, the brewer, everything that had happened. The brewer was overjoyed but could scarcely believe his ears. 'Seeing is believing,' he said. 'Seeing is believing.'

So next day Tom and his master and most of the townsfolk of King's Lynn went out into the marsh. They came to the place where Tom had met the giant, and there Tom showed him the head, and the gold and silver in the cave. They all laughed and leaped for joy, for the giant had been a great terror and threat to them all.

The news of how Tom Hickathrift had killed a giant spread up and down the country. Many people came to see the dead giant and his cave; everyone lit bonfires; and Tom was even more respected than before.

Tom took possession of the cave and its contents, and everyone said he deserved twice as much. Then he pulled down the cave and, with the rocks, built a fine house on the same site. Tom gave some of the giant's land to the poor as common land; the rest he divided into fields, and grew crops, to support himself and his old mother, Jane Hickathrift.

Tom had won a name far and wide and became the most influential man in the district. People called him Mr Hickathrift, and feared his anger just as much as they had feared the giant before. He had manservants and maidservants, he made a deer park, and erected a church dedicated to St James, because he had killed the giant on that saint's feast day. So Tom lived a fine and happy life, visited now and then by his friend the tinker, until the end of his days.

Round the coasts of Britain, where the tidal rivers ebb and flow; on the miles of salt marshes that reach lonely and forsaken like a grey garland of autumn flowers floating in the tide; crouched by the winding creeks that crawl up into the land fed by sluicing tides; by forgotten little harbours of the south coast and the drowned lands where a sea-wall has been breached, and the hungry sea has swallowed back the land that has been won from it through the centuries by the puny ingenuity of man – there you will find him.

You will find him, too, in the damp gloaming of a winter evening; on the forsaken and windswept meal marshes and cockle strands of the Norfolk coast, where the east wind blows for half the year and the bones of wrecked ships strew the sandbanks and the great saddleback gulls cry; where the white thunder of surf for ever forms a rhythmic backcloth of sound, and the seals bark on the long moonlight nights of autumn when the first of the wigeon rafts float into the zos beds on the flooding tides; on the bitter winter marshes of the Wash, where once the great fenland, unhampered and unchecked by the sea-walls, bred wildfowl that darkened the sky in their myriads and the spreading waters reached half across England; by all the sea-washed walls and gull-haunted marshes of our shore. Yes – there you will find him, the shore shooter, the man who finds his 'game' below the level of the high tide sea, between the marks of the highest tides and the lowest tides, on the sea marshes and the mud, and on the sand and shingle beside the sea.

ALAN SAVORY

The Wildman

✤

Don't ask me my name. I've heard you have names. I have no name.

✤

They say this is how I was born. A great wave bored down a river, and at the mouth of the river it ran up against a great wave of the sea. The coupled waves kicked like legs and whirled like arms and swayed like hips; sticks in the water snapped like bones and the seaweed bulged like gristle and muscle. In this way the waves rose. When they fell, I was there.

✤

My home is water as your home is earth. I rise to the surface to breathe air, I glide down through the darkening rainbow.

The water sleeks my hair as I swim. And when I stand on the sea-bed, the currents comb my waving hair; my whole body seems to ripple.

✛

Each day I go to the land for food. I swim to the shore, I'm careful not to be seen. Small things, mice, shrews, moles, I like them to eat. I snuffle and grub through the growth and undergrowth and grab them, and squeeze the warm blood out of them, and chew them.

✛

Always before sunset I'm back in the tugging, chuckling, sobbing water. Then the blue darkness that comes down over the sea comes inside me too. I feel heavy until morning. If I stayed too long on the land I might be found, lying there, heavy, unable even to drag myself back to the water.

✛

My friends are seals. They dive as I do, and swim as I do. Their hair is like my hair. I sing songs with their little ones. They've shown me their secret place, a dark grotto so deep that I howled for the pain of the water pressing round me there and rose to the surface, gasping for air. My friends are the skimming plaice and the flickering eel and the ticklish trout. My friends are all the fishes.

✛

As I swam near the river mouth, something caught my legs and tugged at them. I tried to push it away with my hands and it caught my hands and my arms too. I kicked; I flailed; I couldn't escape. I was dragged through the water, up out of the darkness into the indigo, the purple, the pale blue. I was lifted into the air, the sunlight, and down into a floating thing.

✢

Others. There were others in it, others, others as I am. But
their faces were not covered with hair. They had very little
hair I could see except on their heads, but they were covered
with animal skins and furs. When they saw me they were
afraid and trembled and backed away, and one fell into the
water.

✢

I struggled and bit but I was caught in the web they had
made. They took me to land and a great shoal gathered round
me there. Then they carried me in that web to a great high
place of stone and tipped me out into a gloomy grotto.

✢

One of them stayed by me and kept making noises; I couldn't
understand him. I could tell he was asking me things. I would
have liked to ask him things. How were you born? Why do
you have so little hair? Why do you live on land? I looked at
him, I kept looking at him, and when the others came back, I
looked at them: their hairless hands, their legs, their shining
eyes. There were so many of them almost like me, and I've
never once seen anyone in the sea like me.

✢

They brought me two crossed sticks. Why? What are they?
They pushed them into my face, they howled at me. One of
them smacked my face with his hand. Why was that? It hurt.
Then another with long pale hair came and wept tears over
me. I licked my lips; the tears tasted like the sea. Was this one
like me? Did this one come from the sea? I put my arms
round its waist but it shrieked and pushed me away.

✢

They brought me fish to eat. I wouldn't eat fish. Later they brought me meat; I squeezed it until it was dry and then I ate it.

✤

I was taken out into sunlight, down to the river mouth. The rippling, rippling water. It was pink and lilac and grey; I shivered with longing at the sight of it. I could see three rows of webs spread across the river from bank to bank. Then they let me go, they let me dive into the water. It coursed through my long hair. I laughed and passed under the first web and the second web and the third web. I was free. But why am I only free away from those who are like me, with those who are not like me? Why is the sea my home?

✤

They were all shouting and waving their arms, and jumping up and down at the edge of the water. They were all calling out across the grey wavelets. Why? Did they want me to go back after all? Did they want me to be their friend?

✤

I wanted to go back, I wanted them as friends. So I stroked back under the webs again and swam to the sandy shore. They fell on me then, and twisted my arms, and hurt me. I howled. I screamed. They tied long webs round me and more tightly round me, and carried me back to the place of stone, and threw me into the gloomy grotto.

✤

I bit through the webs. I slipped through the window bars. It was almost night and the blue heaviness was coming into me. I staggered away, back to the water, the waiting dark water.

To pluck the first primrose that appears in the garden in spring and take it into the house is believed to be an unlucky omen for the family. Into farmhouses the carrying of a single flower or a few is sometimes very strongly resented. It is said if the first primroses brought into a farmhouse be less than thirteen, so many eggs only will each hen or goose hatch during the season. A clergyman in East Norfolk was called upon not many years since to decide a quarrel between two old women, arising from one of them having given a single primrose to her neighbour's child, for the purpose of making her hens hatch but one chicken from each set of eggs that season.

JOHN GLYDE

The Green Mist

✤

'Have you carried the light?'

'I have,' said the woman. 'Every day at sundown. I've lit it and carried it round both rooms.'

'What about the words?'

'I've spoken the words.'

'And the blood?'

'I have,' the woman said fiercely. 'Every night I've smeared it on the doorstep to scare away the horrors.'

But still the girl lay ill. One by one each neighbour called with all the same questions; pretty and ramping as she was, caring as she was, they all loved her next to their own daughters. In the back room she lay, never feeling better and slowly getting worse. No medicine cured her, no kind words

cheered her for long, and people said she must be in the power of the bogles.

'She's white and waffling,' said the woman, 'like a bag of bones. And it's almost spring waking.'

The low house moaned. The wind rushed over the fen, vaulted the dykes, and keened in the village.

✣

Day followed day and the girl grew whiter and sillier. She was no more able to stand on her own feet than a baby. She could only lie at the window, watching winter creep away.

'It's creeping,' said the woman.

'Oh mother,' the girl kept saying over and over again, 'if only I could wake the spring with you again. If only I could wake the spring, maybe the green mist would make me strong and well, like the trees and the flowers and the young corn.'

'You'll come to the spring waking,' said the woman. 'You'll come and grow as straight and strong as ever.'

'If only,' said the girl, lying at the window.

But day after day the girl grew whiter and more wan. She looked like a snowflake melting in the sun. And day after day winter crept past; it was almost spring.

Anxiously the girl waited. But she felt so weak and so sick that she knew she would never be able to walk to the fields, and crumble bread and sprinkle salt on them with her mother and all her friends.

'I'll lift you over the doorstep,' the woman said. 'I swear I will, and you can toss out the bread with your own poor thin hands.'

'If the green mist doesn't come in the morning, I won't be able to wait. Not any longer. The soil is calling me. The seeds swelling and bursting now will bloom over my head.'

'No,' said the woman.

'I know it,' said the girl. 'And yet, if I could see the spring wake again . . .' Gravely she stared at the little garden that lay between the low house and the lane. 'If only I could,' she said urgently, 'I swear I'd ask no more than to live as long as one of those cowslips that grow by our gate each year.'

'Quiet!' cried the woman.

The girl looked at her, unblinking.

'Have you no sense? They're all around. You know they can hear you, the bogles.'

But the dawn of the next day brought the green mist.

✤

The mist grew out of the ground and as the gathering light gave colour to everything, the people of the village could see that it was green.

Silently, the mist lifted and fell and lifted, almost luminous. It swayed and reached out its long arms and wrapped itself round everything – low fen houses and the people living in them, trunks of trees and their topmost branches, the church spire. The green mist wove mysterious patterns over the fields and pressed itself against the side of the dyke. It was as green as grass, and fragrant as spring flowers.

The villagers got ready and met to go down to the fields, every man and woman and child who could walk; they all held bread and salt. But not the girl; she could not walk. Her mother took her from her bed and, despite her own aching bones, carried her across the room and over the doorstep, as she had promised.

The girl leaned against a door post, looking into the green mist. She looked and looked and smiled. It was everything and nothing, and beckoning.

'Take this,' said the woman, standing at her side. She gave the girl bread.

The girl crumbled the bread and cast it out a little way from the doorstep.

'This,' said the woman.

The girl took the salt and cast that, too. Then she murmured the old words that were spoken each spring, the strange queer words that everyone said and no one understood.

The woman took a deep long breath and gave a grunt of satisfaction. The girl's eyes were brown, with orange irises. She smiled and, unblinking, she looked at the garden, wrapped in green. She looked at the gate where the cowslips grew.

Then her mother carried her back to her bed by the window. All morning the girl slept. Then, like a baby, she slept all afternoon. Her face was unlined and untroubled. She dreamed of warm summer days and gathering flowers, the laughter of friends.

❖

Whether or not it was the green mist, the girl began to grow stronger and prettier from that day forward. When the sun shone, she got up from her bed and soon left the low house. She flitted about like a will-o'-the-wisp. She danced and sang in the sunlight, as if its warmth were her life.

And the girl went visiting from house to house. All the people of the village loved her, and opened their doors wide and welcome, and felt well to see her well.

When it was cold, or late in the evening, the girl still looked very white and wan. She crouched close to the fire, shaking. But after the spring sowing, she was able to walk with her friends along the lane, and collect flat stones, and lay bread and salt on them to get a good harvest. And when there was not one cloud in the sky for the first week in April, she and her friends trooped down to the fields with buckets; the girl spilt water in the four corners of each field and asked for rain.

By the time the cowslips had opened early in May, the girl had become strangely beautiful; her friends looked at her and thought they could almost see through her; she laughed often enough, but often she was silent, and they wondered what she was thinking. They all knew each other like brother and sister, living as they did a few yards apart in the middle of the great empty marsh; but now they felt that they did not quite know her, and were almost afraid of her.

Every morning the girl knelt by the cowslips at the garden gate. She watered and tended them, and danced beside them in the sunlight.

'Leave them alone!' the woman called.

The girl took no notice.

'Let them be!' ordered the woman, coming out of the low house, abrupt and anxious. 'Leave them alone, or I'll pull them up.'

Then the girl stopped dancing and looked at the woman strangely. 'Mother,' she said in a soft low voice, 'don't even pick one of those flowers unless you're tired of me.'

The woman pressed her lips together.

'They'll fade soon enough,' said the girl, 'soon enough, yes, as you know.'

✢

Early one evening a boy from the village stopped by the gate to gossip with the girl and the woman. The sun cast long shadows and a light, slight wind breathed around them: just the time for passing time!

The boy picked a flower and twirled it between his fingers as they talked – talked of the birth of a baby, and a mid-summer marriage; talked of the fen that was full of prying bogles and horrible boggarts; talked of the need to improve the dyke. They had no thought or knowledge of the world and its worries beyond.

Out across the marsh the wind started forward. It sprang over the dyke, tousled and interrupted them.

'That's blowing,' said the boy, and he dropped the flower.

The girl suddenly tightened and trembled. 'You,' she said, staring at the boy's feet. 'Did you pull that cowslip?' She looked strange and white, and pressed her right hand over her heart.

The boy glanced down; then he stooped and scooped it up. He looked at the girl, thinking he had never really noticed quite how lovely and different she was. 'Here you are,' he said, offering her the flower, grinning.

The girl took the cowslip. She stared at the flower, and at the boy, and everything about her; at the green trees, and the sprouting grass, and the yellow blooms, and up at the golden shining sun. Then, all at once, shrinking as if the sunlight that she loved so much were burning her, the girl turned and ran into the low house. She said nothing; she only gave a sort of cry, like a poor dumb beast in pain. And she caught the cowslip close against her heart.

✣

The girl lay huddled on her bed. She did not move. She did not move at all. She stared at the flower in her hand as it faded, hour by hour.

'Come,' said the woman, and offered her food, drink, and friendly talk.

But the girl said nothing, and night came on. She never spoke again.

At dawn, lying on the bed, there was only a white dead shrunken thing, with a shrivelled cowslip in its hand. The woman covered it with a quilt, and thought of the beautiful laughing girl, dancing like a bird in the sunshine, down by the yellow nodding flowers. Only yesterday, she thought. 'Yesterday,' she whispered to herself.

The bogles had heard her and given the girl her wish. She had bloomed with the cowslips and faded with the first of them.

'It's all true,' the woman whispered, 'true as death.'

Cromer crabs.
Runton dabs;
Beeston babies,
Sherringham ladies;
Weybourne witches;
Salthouse ditches;
Langham fairmaids,
Blakeney bulldogs,
Morsta dodmen,
Binham bulls,
Stiffkey blues;
Wells bitefingers,
And the Blakeney people
Stand on the steeple,
And crack hazel-nuts
With a five-farthing beetle.

TRADITIONAL

dodmen: snails
blues: mussels
Wells bitefingers: a Wells sailor is said to have
   bitten off a drowned man's finger to get his ring.

The Callow Pit Coffer

✤

'Keep away from Callow Pit,' said Thor, the old cottar, and stabbed at the fire with his stick.

Thor's three sons, Jakke, and Keto and the little cripple Simpkin had heard his warning before. 'That place, it's haunted! It's unnatural!' He had told them a hundred times if he had told them once.

And Simpkin shivered.

But Jakke and Keto glanced at one another; their eyes shifted with some deep secret only they shared.

Jakke was the elder brother, ill at ease with other men, a skinflint with words. Yet he loved animals of every kind, and hated to see them suffer the slings of winter; and he was always gentle with Simpkin.

Keto was the rogue everyone liked, the practical joker, the poacher who pinched Sir Jocelin's rabbits and hares and, best

of all, his fleet deer; he was red-haired as a fox.

But Jakke and Keto had things in common too: they were both big men, fine wrestlers; they were both brave; danger excited them.

'There are spirits and phantoms at Callow Pit,' said Thor. 'And that's where the headless horseman rides.' He jabbed again at the fire. 'If you have to pass it, keep your mouths shut. Remember the saying, *if you don't bother them with words, they won't bother you.*'

Callow Pit lay under the shadow of a bald hill, in a gloomy hollow where four ways met. One day the water rose in it high, the next it sank mysteriously low. And if you peered into it, the water was so dark you could not see your own face. The stories about it scared Thor and all the other people of Southwood.

'Face to face to face to face, you only give, I only take,' warbled the simpleton Odda. But no one listened to him, neither Thor and his sons, nor anyone else; perhaps he was wiser than they knew.

'I *saw* the headless horseman,' whispered Edmund, the young cottar, to Emma, his bride. 'I saw him as he galloped up from the Spon. He rides past Southwood church, skirting the graveyard, on and on, and disappears near Callow Pit.'

Everyone knew Callow Pit was evil. Its black eye watched the world, unblinking. The two oak trees beside it had been struck by lightning, and withered and died.

But everyone in Southwood knew another thing.

'Gold,' said Thor, 'at the bottom of the pit.' He leaned forward on his stick, nodding his grizzled head, and confided, 'In an iron coffer, gold and silver.'

'Like the sun and the moon,' sighed Simpkin.

'Like your hair,' whispered Edmund to Emma, in their hut.

'How did it get there?' asked Emma.

'Some people say Danes left it there and never lived to

collect it; others say King Edmund sank it there in case the Danes should get it; and some are sure our grandfathers' fathers hid it when Duke William came. Where did it come from? Nobody knows.' Edmund paused. 'But God knows, we could do with it now, with that devil Sir Jocelin for lord, and the worst of winter still to come.'

'Go on, then!' said Emma, and she opened her blue eyes. 'If you love me, go and get it.'

Then she smiled, and Edmund smiled too. But he felt disquieted all the same, and wished she had not suggested it.

Later, they prayed together: 'Save us from starving and freezing, O God; O God, give us our daily bread.'

And Odda, the simpleton, in his hut, said to himself, 'Brr! Poor Odda's heart is gold, but the devil's in him.'

The north wind blew over the hill and through the hamlet. Freezing blasts carried off everyone's words.

✛

The very same idea that disquieted Edmund was already at work in the minds of Jakke and Keto. For that was their secret. They were planning to go to Callow Pit by night, and fish for gold. Had Thor known their intention, he would have tried to stop them, and sworn by St William of Norwich that no good could come of it.

'This story, that story about Callow Pit!' said Jakke contemptuously. 'I don't believe in them. Old men's chatter! Old wives' tales!' His eyes were the colour of iron. 'If there's gold, I must get it. Think! We could walk to Norwich fair, buy horses there, ride home laden with salted meat and corn . . .'

'If you go, I go,' interrupted Keto. His scalp tingled at the idea, for he half believed the stories himself. But the danger only made him all the more eager. 'There'd be enough,' he exclaimed, 'for us, and father and Simpkin, enough for everyone in Southwood.'

'All right,' agreed Jakke. 'The two of us! Tonight, when nobody's about.'

And so they put their heads together and laid their plans, down to the smallest detail.

As soon as they were sure that Thor and Simpkin were asleep, Jakke and Keto crept out of the smoky hut. Icy fingers of air burned through their clothing.

'Listen!' whispered Jakke.

In his own hut, Odda was singing softly: 'Beware, I'm an eye, I see you coming. I'll be silent, I'll say nothing. Please say nothing, heal me, heal me.' And his voice was pure as the single bird which defied the darkness and the cold, and cheeped from its perch in the alder tree.

Jakke cocked his head to one side, listening.

'Come on,' Keto whispered urgently. 'We haven't got all night.'

'We have,' said Jakke.

Then the brothers stole away from Southwood under the stars and the bruised moon. They hurried past the hut where Edmund and Emma lay asleep, strode across the common land and round the two open fields, towards the manor of Sir Jocelin de Neville. With them they brought a long leather thong, and an oak staff with an iron hook. All they needed were Sir Jocelin's ladders.

Jakke and Keto stepped through the great gateway and across the deserted courtyard. Their boots crunched on the gravel.

'Quick!' said Jakke.

'There!' said Keto.

They sprang across the yard and snatched up the ladders from beneath the hay loft.

'Come on!' urged Jakke.

At once he and Keto hoisted the ladders between them, one on either shoulder. And as Sir Jocelin's wolfhounds, tethered in their kennels, began to bark, they loped across the yard and under the gateway arch again, and set off for the cross-ways, and Callow Pit.

'Well!' said Jakke. 'Are you ready?'

Keto nodded.

'Remember . . .' said Jakke.

'What's that?' said Keto stiffening. The nape of his neck tingled.

'What?' said Jakke. 'I didn't hear anything.'

'Hooves,' said Keto. 'The drumming of hooves.'

A small buffeting wind had got up, a night wind from nowhere, and with it a few clouds that scudded before the moon. It was darker than it was before.

'I said he hadn't got all night,' whispered Keto.

Jakke scowled, and put two fingers to his lips. 'Remember,' he said in a low voice. 'Quiet now.'

So they came to the hollow where four ways met. The first way led to Southwood, the second to the sea, the third lost itself in a thicket, and the fourth plunged through a cutting where demons lived.

The bald back of the hill sheltered Callow Pit. The water was still. It looked like pitch. The grey torsos of the blasted oaks leaned over it.

The two brothers stared down at the pool, then stared at each other. Now they were filled with doubts, and all the stories about Callow Pit crowded into their minds . . .

Then Jakke moved forward, and Keto followed him. He had to, for he was carrying the other end of the ladders! At the pit's edge they laid the ladders end to end and bound them tightly together with a leather thong.

Jakke motioned to Keto to hold one end and, grasping the other, he edged his way round the pool. When he was standing opposite Keto, each lowered his end on to the damp soil; they had bridged Callow Pit.

Now Keto walked round the pool and handed Jakke the staff, and at once Jakke stepped out, a rung at a time, over Callow Pit. One rung, two rungs, three rungs, four rungs. Five rungs – the bank already looked a long way off. Keto followed two rungs behind him. The ladders held firm. They were stout, and strongly bound.

Now Jakke grasped the staff more firmly; his knuckles gleamed like ivory. He drew in his breath and plunged the hook into the water.

A raven screeched, starting from its hideout in the oak stump. Jakke leaned forward and prodded the bottom of the pit. Nothing! He drew the dripping staff out of the water and awkwardly turned about. Then he plunged it in a second time.

The result was just the same.

So the two brothers stepped forward again until Keto stood in the very middle of the pit. His blood whirled; he felt giddy. He took the iron-hooked staff from Jakke and rammed it into the water.

'Cluung!' They heard it directly; the clang of metal against metal underneath the water.

Keto drew in his breath. He went down on one knee and probed more carefully. It *feels* like the coffer, he thought. It's the right shape. It *is* the coffer!

Suddenly, the iron hook snagged. Keto pulled at the staff; some force had caught against it. He pulled harder, and harder, and the weight began to move.

Then Jakke crouched forward and gripped the staff as well. He tugged with all his strength. The ladders groaned. And slowly, swaying like drunkards, the two brothers lifted up and out of the water, inch by inch, a dripping, crusted iron coffer.

They gasped at it: the great lock on it; the massive ring in its lid which had snagged their hook.

Carefully, they lowered it on to the ladders, and the ladders creaked and complained more angrily, and sagged at the centre.

Oh the gold and the silver, thought Keto. His mind sang like a bird. Food for us, Thor and Simpkin, for everyone else . . . not one piece for Sir Jocelin . . .

Jakke tapped Keto on the shoulder and took the staff from him. He slipped it through the ring so that they could sling the coffer between them. Then each brother put one end of the staff over his shoulder. They were rich, and ready to go.

Keto could have climbed to the moon. The stars in the sky seemed to spray like sparks above his head. 'We've got it!' he shouted. 'We've got it, and the devil himself can't get it from us now!'

Then at once a yellowish mist surged up from the water, and swirled angrily about them. It caught at their throats; they coughed and spluttered and choked. Birds shrieked out of the stillness of night; the air was full of flapping of wings. Wolves howled. Grass blades stiffened. The hackles of all natural things rose at the unnatural.

'Quick!' yelled Jakke. 'Quick, Keto!'

It was too late. Out of the water thrust a hideous black hand, then a huge black arm.

The unearthly hand clawed at the ladder; its nails were like spikes. Keto bared his teeth. 'Don't let go,' he growled, furiously determined not to lose the coffer.

Jakke crushed his end of the staff in his grip. The ladders groaned and curved like a crossbow; cold water gripped their ankles.

Then the arm wound round the coffer, and yanked it. Jakke and Keto lurched forward on their toes, rocked back on to their heels. They refused to let go.

'Pull! Pull!' urged Keto. 'Pull!'

The yellow vapour wrapped them in its hundred arms; the oak staff held firm, stronger than them all.

The brothers pulled again, with the strength of ten men. Then metal screamed; the coffer and the ring in its lid were torn apart.

Jakke and Keto cried out as they fell backwards into the water; and the coffer, the coffer hit the surface of the pool with a colossal splash. It disappeared from sight.

✧

Sodden and shivering, still holding the staff and ring, Jakke and Keto sat on the damp earth, a little way off from the pit. At last, Jakke broke the silence. 'Keto!' he said. 'Keto! Keto!'

And Keto shook his head dumbly.

So the coffer they had not, because Keto had forgotten the saying, and spoken; but they had the ring for their pains – the massive iron ring as a proof of their exploit.

Jakke and Keto looked at it and fingered it, wonderingly. Yellow tinged the pale green of the east; all was not lost even if the coffer was lost.

Jakke stood up and stretched. 'We should go now,' he said.

'The ladders,' said Keto in a small voice, and his arms ached.

'Confound the ladders!' said Jakke.

'Where have you been?' demanded Thor as soon as Jakke and Keto stepped into the hut. 'What's that ring?'

'We'll tell you,' said Keto.

'You will,' said Thor. 'You're soaking. Where have you been?'

'Callow Pit,' said Jakke.

'You see this ring?' said Keto, lifting it between his hands like a crown.

'What is it?' muttered Thor uneasily.

So Jakke and Keto told them the whole story, from first to last. And Thor, who had begun by being angry and fearful, ended by being fearful and proud.

Simpkin, too, glowed with pride at the daring of his brothers. But there was an ache in his heart because he had not gone with them, and never would.

Then Thor hurried out in the sharp, early morning air. He was full of the story, anxious to tell anyone and everyone, and as quickly as he could.

He was not disappointed. In the two fields that day, and over food, and in the smoky firelight, Jakke and Keto and Callow Pit were the only topic of conversation.

Edmund and Emma listened to the story standing shoulder to shoulder. As it unfolded, their eyes opened wider and wider, and Emma wished she had not teased Edmund and dared him to go to Callow Pit.

When the tale was told in the hearing of Odda, he sat bolt upright and listened most attentively: and later he was heard to say in a sad voice: 'I am what I was, alas, alas. Dark's still in me; dispossess me.'

❖

'What shall we do with the ring?' said Keto.

'I'm not having it in here,' said Thor. 'It's an evil thing. Throw it away.'

'Why should it be evil?' said Jakke.

'It's a proof,' said Keto.

'It's a warning,' Thor growled.

'I know,' said Simpkin. 'You could fix it to the church door. People will see it there, now and always . . .'

Jakke and Keto nodded.

'And if *you* are right,' Simpkin said to his father, 'then its evil will be useless on sacred ground. You can commend it to the mercy of the saints.'

Simpkin's suggestion pleased them all. And so, in due course, after Thor had explained their purpose to the priest, the massive ring was secured to the door of St Edmund's Church.

Anyone could go to see it there, and everyone did. Pedlars and pilgrims, travelling quacks and tinkers came to visit the church at Southwood.

Then they visited the tavern; they drank mead, they drank ale, they ate meat pies. And that put gold into the pockets of the people of Southwood, perhaps even as much as was in the coffer.

But after Jakke's and Keto's experience, no one went too close to Callow Pit again. The people who had to walk or ride along the four ways did so as quickly as they could; they had no wish whatsoever to risk their lives for gold.

An Irishman was hired by a Yarmouth maltster to help in loading his ship. As the vessel was about to sail, the Irishman cried out from the quay, 'Captain, I lost your shovel overboard, but I cut a big notch in the rail fence round the stern, just where it went down, so you will find it when you come back.'

TRADITIONAL

A Coggeshall Calendar

✛

It was April and the good people of Coggeshall were worried. Some of them were worried because there was too much wind, and some because there was too little.

'The black plague!' cried one old woman. 'The wind keeps blowing it in.'

And so she and her friends strung clothes-lines from tree to tree across the four roads leading into Coggeshall.

'The black plague!' cried the old women. 'We must keep it out!'

And they hung thick grey blankets over all the clothes-lines.

But the wind that worried the old women was not strong enough to please the two millers in the village.

'There's just not enough wind for us both,' said one.

'We've got one mill too many,' said the other. 'That's the truth of it.'

'You know what we must do?' the first miller said.

Then the two men walked and talked and, in the end, they shook hands and pulled down one of the mills.

✣

It was July and the good people of Coggeshall were worried. Some of them were worried because it was not warm enough, and some because it was too wet.

'If we don't do something about it, there'll be no harvest this year,' said one man.

'And what's more,' said another, 'we'll all get washed away.'

So one group of villagers busied themselves in the orchards, lighting bonfires under all the plum-trees to help the fruit to ripen.

But another group kept watch over the rising stream.

'It's about to break its banks.'

'Remember what happened last time?'

'The flood, yes, the flood. Poor old Amy, she had to pull down her staircase.'

'Yes, otherwise the water would have got upstairs.'

So they collected as many willow-hurdles and hazel-hurdles as they could, and put up a good, strong fence across the meadow between the stream and the village.

✣

It was October and the good people of Coggeshall were worried because a rabid dog had bitten a wheelbarrow.

'That'll be the end of it,' said one woman.

'It'll go mad,' said her friend.

So the two of them hurriedly trundled the barrow into a garden shed, and chained it up, and locked it in.

✧

It was December and the good people of Coggeshall were worried. All year they had been building a new church and everyone had lent a hand – man, woman and child. But they had forgotten to put in any windows.

'We'll have to do it the hard way,' said the masterbuilder.

Hearing this, a large band of villagers went back to their homes in search of hampers and wheelbarrows – but not the barrow that was still in quarantine.

Back in the churchyard, they opened their hampers to catch the sunlight. Then, at a signal from the masterbuilder, they shut them up tight and wheeled them into the church.

When they opened their hampers again, and found no sunlight inside them, the villagers were very puzzled.

✧

It was February and the good people of Coggeshall were worried. They were worried because they had not built their fine new church in exactly the right place.

'There's nothing for it,' said the masterbuilder. 'We'll have to give it a push.'

Freezing as it was, the masterbuilder and his companions all took off their coats and laid them on the ground outside the east end of the church. Then they walked round to the west end and put their right shoulders against the wall.

'Ready?' said the masterbuilder.

Then they grunted and they shoved, and when they judged they had moved the church to its right position, they walked round to the east end again to pick up their coats.

But their coats had gone. Every single one of them.

'Darn!'

'Drat!'

'Where are they?'

'They can't have got up and walked away.'

'You know what we've done,' said the masterbuilder, pointing at the foot of the east wall. 'What noodles we are! We've pushed the church right over them.'

'Ah! That's all right, then,' said his companions, much relieved.

Then they all trooped into the church to collect their coats.

✢

It was April and the good people of Coggeshall were worried. A whole year had passed by and they hadn't even noticed it. A whole year, and it was time to begin again.

Come, brethren of the water, and let us all assemble,
To treat upon this matter, which makes us quake and
    tremble;
For we shall rue it, if't be true, that Fens be undertaken,
And where we feed in Fen and Reed, they'll feed both
    Beef and Bacon.

They'll sow both beans and oats, where never man yet
    thought it,
Where men did row in boats, ere undertakers bought it:
But, Ceres, thou, behold us now, let wild oats be their
    venture,
Oh let the frogs and miry bogs destroy where they
    do enter.

Behold the great design, which they do now determine,
Will make our bodies pine, a prey to crows and vermine:
For they do mean all Fens to drain, and waters
    overmaster,
All will be dry, and we must die, 'cause Essex calves
    want pasture . . .

The feather'd fowls have wings, to fly to other nations;
But we have no such things, to help our
    transportations;
We must give place (oh grievous case) to horned beasts
    and cattle,
Except that we can all agree to drive them out by
    battle.

ANONYMOUS

Tiddy Mun

✤

Before the dykes were dug, there was marsh and more marsh, as far as the eye could see.

The whole placed teemed with boggarts and will-o'-the-wykes and other evil creatures. In the darkness, hands without arms reached out of the water and beckoned; voices of the dead cried and moaned all night long; and goblins danced on the tussocks. There were witches too; they mounted the great black snags of peat, and turned them into snakes and raced about on them in the water. No wonder people stayed indoors after nightfall. The marsh was no place to be after dark, and when some man did have to make his way home along the marsh-paths by lamplight, he shook with fright – his skin crawled with terror from the crown of his head to the tips of his toes.

But there was another spirit living in the marshes. He had no name and everyone called him Tiddy Mun.

Tiddy Mun lived in the deep and dark green waterholes that never moved from dawn to dusk. But when the evening mist dipped and lifted and dipped over the marsh, Tiddy Mun rose to the surface and hoisted himself on to some marsh path. He went creeping through the darkness, limpelty lobelty, like a dear little old grandfather with long white hair and a long white beard, all matted and tangled; he hobbled along, limpelty lobelty, wearing a grey gown so that people could scarcely make him out from the mist. His movement was the sound of running water and the sough of the wind, and his laugh was like the screech of a peewit.

No one was scared of Tiddy Mun like they were of the boggarts. He wasn't wicked and chancy like the water-wraiths; and he wasn't white and creepy like the dead hands. All the same, it was kind of scary to sit in front of your own fire and then hear a screeching laugh right outside the door, a screeching laugh passing by in a skirl of wind and water.

Tiddy Mun did no one any harm and there were times when he did people a really good turn. When rain fell day after day, and the water level rose in the marshes and crept up to the doors, and soaked the bundles of straw strewn over people's floors, a whole family – father and mother and children – would go out into the darkness or the night of the new moon. They stared out over the marshes and called out together, 'Tiddy Mun, without a name, Tiddy Mun, the waters are washing through.'

The children clung to their mother, and their mother clung to her husband, and they all stood shaking and shivering in the darkness. Then they heard the peewit-screech over the swamp. That was Tiddy Mun's reply. Sure enough, in the morning the water level had dropped and the bundles of straw were dry again. And that was Tiddy Mun's doing.

Then outsiders moved in, rich farmers and surveyors and, after them, gangs of Dutchmen. They said it was high time the marshes were drained, and told fine stories about how the mist would lift once and for all, and how the swamps would be turned into fields, and how no one would suffer from marsh-fever ever again.

The marshmen were against that. They knew the cause of their aches and complaints: if they were not shaking with fear because of the boggarts, as often as not they were shaking with the fevers and agues that rose from the marshes. But they were used to them and used to the look of the place; it was their home. 'Bad is bad,' they said, 'but meddling is worse.'

Above all, the marshmen took against the Dutchmen who had come over the sea to dig and drain around them. They wouldn't give them food, or bedding, or even greet them in passing. Everyone muttered it would be an ill day for them all when the marshes were drained and Tiddy Mun was angered.

All the same, the marshmen were unable to do anything about it. The Dutchmen dug and drew the water off; they emptied the water-holes so that they were as dry as two-year-old Mothering Cakes. The dykes got longer and longer, and deeper and deeper; the water ran away, and ran away down to the river, and the whole soppy, quivering swamp was turned into firm land. The marshmen saw that the soft black bog would soon be replaced by green fields.

Then, one day, one of the Dutchmen disappeared. And, soon afterwards, a second one followed him. They were spirited away! The work gangs searched for them and searched for them, but not a shadow of them was ever seen again. The marshmen nodded; they knew well enough they would never find them, not if they searched until the golden Beasts of Judgement came roaring and ramping over the land to fetch away sinners.

The old marshmen wagged their heads and their children wagged their tongues and said, 'That's what comes of crossing Tiddy Mun!'

But the outsiders, the rich farmers and surveyors, were not to be put off. They brought in one work gang after another and although Tiddy Mun drowned many of them, the work of draining the marshes slowly progressed. The marshmen were helpless and, soon enough, there were worse disasters.

The marshmen's own cows began to pine, their pigs starved and their ponies went lame. The children fell sick, lambs died, and new milk curdled. Thatched roofs fell in, walls burst at the seams, and everything was arsy-versy.

At first the marshmen couldn't think who or what had caused such trouble. They said it was the work of the witches or the goblins. They turned on Sally, the old woman with the evil eye who could charm dead men out of their graves, and ducked her in the horsepond until she was more dead than alive; they all said the Lord's Prayer backwards; and they spat to the east to keep the goblins away. But it was no good. Tiddy Mun himself was angry and upset with them all.

What could they do? Little children sickened in their mothers' arms; all the poor white faces never brightened but became more and more wan. Their fathers sat and puffed their pipes and their mothers cried over their little innocent babies, lying so white and smiling and peaceful. Tiddy Mun's anger was like a frost that comes and kills the prettiest flowers.

The marshmen's hearts were heavy and their stomachs were empty, what with the sickness and the bad harvest and this, that and the other. They knew something must be done, and done soon, before it was too late and they were all dead and gone.

Then one man thought of the old times. 'Remember before the delving?' he said. 'Remember how, when the waters rose, we went out into the night under the new moon, and called out to Tiddy Mun?'

'He heard us then,' said another man, 'and he did as we asked him.'

'Let's call on him again,' said the first man.

The marshmen talked. They thought that if they called out to Tiddy Mun, to show they wished him well and would give him back the water if only they could, he might lift the curse on them all and forgive them again.

Before darkness fell on the night of the next new moon, there was a great gathering of marshfolk down by the largest of the dykes across the marsh. They came in threes and fours, jumping at every sough of the wind and starting at every snag of stranded peat. They need not have worried. The poor old boggarts and will-o'-the-wykes had been entirely dug out, all the swamp-bogles had followed the waters and flitted away.

While it slowly grew dark, they all huddled together. They whispered and watched, and kept an eye on the shadows over their shoulders; they listened uneasily to the skirling of the wind and the lip-lap of the running water. And every single one of them – man, woman and child – carried a stoup of fresh water in his hands.

At long last it was night. They all stood on the edge of the dyke, and loudly they all called out together, as if with one voice: 'Tiddy Mun, without a name, here's water for you, water for you, lift your curse.'

Then they tipped the water out of their stoups and into the dyke – splash sploppert!

The marshmen listened, a small scared huddle clinging to one another in the middle of the stillness. They listened to see if Tiddy Mun would answer them; but there was nothing but a great unnatural stillness.

And then, just when they thought it was all in vain, the most terrible whimpering and wailing broke out all around them. It surged to and fro and sounded for all the world like a crowd of little babies crying their hearts out, with no one to comfort them. They sobbed and sobbed themselves almost into silence; and then they began again, louder than ever, wailing and moaning until it made the heart ache to hear them.

Suddenly, one mother after another began to cry out that it was her dead baby, calling on Tiddy Mun to lift the curse and let the marsh children live and grow strong.

Then, out of the dark air overhead, the babies moaned and gently whimpered, as if they recognised their mothers' voices and were trying to find their breasts.

'A little hand touched me,' one woman said.

'Cold lips kissed me,' said another woman.

They all said they felt soft wings fluttering round them as they stood and listened to that mournful greeting.

Then, all at once, there was complete stillness again. The marshmen could hear the water lapping at their feet, and a dog yelping in a distant hut.

And then, out of the river itself, soft and fond came the old peewit-screech. Once and a second time: it was Tiddy Mun.

And the marshmen, they all knew he would lift his curse. How they laughed and shouted and ran and jumped, like a pack of children coming out of school, as they set off home with light hearts and never a thought of the boggarts.

But the marshwomen followed slowly. They were all silent, thinking of their babies. Their arms felt empty and their hearts lonely and weary because of the cold kisses, the fluttering of the little fingers. They wept as they thought of their little babies, drifting to and fro in the moaning of the night wind.

From that day, things began to change and prosper. Sick children got well, cattle chewed the cud and the bacon-pigs fattened. The marshmen earned good money and there was bread in plenty. Tiddy Mun had indeed lifted his curse.

But every new moon, all the marsh folk – men and women and children – went into the darkness and down to the edge of the dyke. There they tipped their stoups into the dyke and cried out, 'Tiddy Mun, without a name, here's water for you, water for you.'

Then out of the river itself, soft and tender and pleased, rose the peewit-screech. And the marshmen went back to their houses, happy and contented.

But one thing is certain. If any man failed to go down to the dyke without good reason, unless he were ill, Tiddy Mun missed him and was angry with him, and laid the curse upon him worse than ever. There was nothing he could do about it until the next new moon, when he went down to the dyke with the others to beg that the curse should be lifted. And when children misbehaved, their parents warned them that Tiddy Mun would spirit them away; they were as good as gold after that, for they all knew the warnings were true enough.

Every marshman knew that little figure, limping by in the mist, all grey and white, screeching like a peewit. But one month, when the marshmen trooped down to the dyke at new moon, and called out to Tiddy Mun, they got no reply. It was the same the next month, and the month after. Without warning, Tiddy Mun had vanished.

Why did he go? Perhaps he was frightened away by all the changes and new machines in Lincolnshire. And where did he go? Perhaps he is here, perhaps he is there, Tiddy Mun. Only listen for the laugh in a skirl of wind and the sound of running water.

During the reign of Richard the Lionheart, a spirit kept appearing in the house of Osborn Bradwell at Dagworth in Suffolk. She talked to his family, sounded like a one-year-old, and her name was Malkin.

To begin with, Osborn's wife and servants were very scared of her, but after a while they got used to her and she made them laugh by describing the things that neighbours did in private and thought that no one else knew about. You could hear Malkin's voice (she spoke in a Suffolk dialect and sometimes in Latin) you could touch her, but you couldn't see her – though just once she was seen by a chambermaid who said she looked like a very small girl, dressed in a white tunic.

Malkin said she had been born at Lavenham. Her mother had carried her into a field and laid her down to sleep in the shade while she worked with the other harvesters. Then a strange woman picked her up and ran off with her. Malkin said she had lived with this woman for seven years; and that after another seven years, she would be able to come home to her own mother and family. She said she wore a cap which made her invisible – and so did the spirits of some other children. Often, she asked Osborn's servants for food and drink; and when they put it out for her on top of an old chest, it simply disappeared.

RALPH OF COGGESHALL

The Dauntless Girl

✛

'Dang it!' said the farmer.

'Why?' said the miller.

'Not a drop left,' the farmer said.

'Not one?' asked the blacksmith, raising his glass and inspecting it. His last inch of whisky glowed like molten honey in the flickering firelight.

'Why not?' said the miller

'You fool!' said the farmer. 'Because the bottle's empty.' He peered into the flames. 'Never mind that though,' he said. 'We'll send out my Mary. She'll go down to the inn and bring us another bottle.'

'What?' said the blacksmith. 'She'll be afraid to go out on such a dark night, all the way down to the village, and all on her own.'

'Never!' said the farmer. 'She's afraid of nothing – nothing live or dead. She's worth all my lads put together.'

The farmer gave a shout and Mary came out of the kitchen. She stood and she listened. She went out into the dark night and in a little time she returned with another bottle of whisky.

The miller and the blacksmith were delighted. They drank to her health, but later the miller said, 'That's a strange thing, though.'

'What's that?' asked the farmer.

'That she should be so bold, your Mary.'

'Bold as brass,' said the blacksmith. 'Out and alone and the night so dark.'

'That's nothing at all,' said the farmer. 'She'd go anywhere, day or night. She's afraid of nothing – nothing live or dead.'

'Words!' said the blacksmith. 'But my, this whisky tastes good.'

'Words nothing,' said the farmer. 'I bet you a golden guinea that neither of you can name anything that girl will not do.'

The miller scratched his head and the blacksmith peered at the golden guinea of whisky in his glass. 'All right,' said the blacksmith. 'Let's meet here again at the same time next week. Then I'll name something Mary will not do.'

✛

Seven days later the blacksmith went to see the priest and borrowed the key of the church door from him. Then he paid a visit to the sexton and showed him the key.

'What do you want with that?' asked the sexton.

'What I want with you,' said the blacksmith, 'is this. I want you to go into the church tonight, just before midnight, and hide yourself in the dead house.'

'Never!' said the sexton.

'Not for half a guinea?' asked the blacksmith.

The old sexton's eyes popped out of his head. 'Dang it!' he said. 'What's that for then?'

'To frighten that brazen farm girl, Mary,' said the blacksmith, grinning. 'When she comes to the dead house, just give a moan or a holler.'

The old sexton's desire for the half guinea was even greater than his fear. He hummed and hawed and at last he agreed to do as the blacksmith asked. Then the blacksmith clumped the sexton on the back with his massive fist and the old sexton coughed. 'I'll see you tomorrow,' said the blacksmith, 'and settle the account. Just before midnight, then! Not a minute later!'

The sexton nodded and the blacksmith strode up to the farm. Darkness was falling and the farmer and the miller were already drinking and waiting for him.

'Well?' said the farmer.

The blacksmith grasped his glass then raised it and rolled the whisky around his mouth.

'Well,' said the farmer. 'Are you or aren't you?'

'This,' said the blacksmith, 'is what your Mary will not do. She won't go into the church alone at midnight . . .'

'No,' said the miller.

'. . . and go to the dead house,' continued the blacksmith, 'and bring back a skull bone. That's what she won't do.'

'Never,' said the miller.

The farmer gave a shout and Mary came out of the kitchen. She stood and she listened; and later, at midnight, she went out into the darkness and walked down to the church.

Mary opened the church door. She held up her lamp and clattered down the steps to the dead house. She pushed open its creaking door and saw skulls and thigh bones and bones of every kind gleaming in front of her. She stooped and picked up the nearest skull bone.

'Let that be!' moaned a muffled voice from behind the dead house door. 'That's my mother's skull bone.'

So Mary put that skull down and picked up another.

'Let that be!' moaned a muffled voice from behind the dead house door. 'That's my father's skull bone.'

So Mary put that skull bone down too and picked up yet another one. And, as she did so, she angrily called out, 'Father or mother, sister or brother, I *must* have a skull bone and that's my last word.' Then she walked out of the dead house, latched the door, and hurried up the steps and back up to the farm.

Mary put the skull bone on the table in front of the farmer. 'There's your skull bone, master,' she said, and started off for the kitchen.

'Wait a minute!' said the blacksmith, and he was grinning and shivering. 'Didn't you hear anything in the dead house, Mary?'

'Yes,' she said. 'Some fool of a ghost called out: "Let that be! That's my mother's skull bone" and "Let that be! That's my father's skull bone."' But I told him straight: "Father or mother, sister or brother, I *must* have a skull bone."'

The miller and the blacksmith stared at Mary and shook their heads.

'So I took one,' said Mary, 'and here it is.' She looked down at the three faces flickering in the firelight. 'After I had locked the door,' she said, 'and climbed the steps, I heard the old ghost hollering and shrieking like mad.'

At once the blacksmith and the miller got to their feet.

'That'll do then, Mary,' said the farmer.

The blacksmith knew the sexton must have been scared out of his wits at being locked inside the dead house. He and his friends hurried down to the church, and clattered down the steps into the dead house. They were too late. They found the old sexton lying stone dead on his face.

'That's what comes of trying to frighten a poor young girl,' said the farmer.

So the blacksmith gave the farmer a golden guinea and the farmer gave it to his Mary.

✛

Mary and her daring were known in every house. And after her visit to the dead house, and the death of the old sexton, her fame spread for miles and miles around.

One day the squire, who lived three villages off, rode up to the farm and asked the farmer if he could talk to Mary.

'I've heard,' said the squire, 'that you're afraid of nothing.'

Mary nodded.

'Nothing live or dead,' said the farmer proudly.

'Listen then!' said the squire. 'Last year my old mother died and was buried. But she will not rest. She keeps coming back into the house, and especially at mealtimes.'

Mary stood and listened.

'Sometimes you can see her, sometimes you can't. And when you can't, you can still see a knife and fork get up off the table and play about where her hands would be.'

'That's a strange thing altogether,' said the farmer.

'Strange and unnatural,' said the squire. 'And now my servants won't stay with me, not one of them. They're all afraid of her.'

The farmer sighed and shook his head. 'Hard to come by, good servants,' he said.

'So,' said the squire, 'seeing as she's afraid of nothing, nothing live or dead, I'd like to ask your girl to come and work with me.'

Mary was pleased at the prospect of such good employment and, sorry as he was to lose her, the farmer saw there was nothing for it but to let her go.

'I'll come,' said the girl. 'I'm not afraid of ghosts. But you ought to take account of that in my wages.'

'I will,' said the squire.

So Mary went back with the squire to be his servant. The first thing she always did was to lay a place for the ghost at table, and she took great care not to let the knife and fork lie criss-cross.

At meals, Mary passed the ghost the meat and vegetables and sauce and gravy. And then she said: 'Pepper, madam?' and 'Salt, madam?'

The ghost of the squire's mother was pleased enough. So things went on the same from day to day until the squire had to go up to London to settle some legal business.

Next morning Mary was down on her knees, cleaning the parlour grate, when she noticed something thin and glimmering push in through the parlour door, which was just ajar; when it got inside the room, the shape began to swell and open out. It was the old ghost.

For the first time, the ghost spoke to the girl. 'Mary,' she said in a hollow voice, 'are you afraid of me?'

'No, madam,' said Mary. 'I've no cause to be afraid of you, for you are dead and I'm alive.'

For a while the ghost looked at the girl kneeling by the parlour grate. 'Mary,' she said, 'will you come down into the cellar with me? You mustn't bring a light – but I'll shine enough to light the way for you.'

So the two of them went down the cellar steps and the ghost shone like an old lantern. When they got to the bottom, they went along a passage, and took a right turn and a left, and then the ghost pointed to some loose tiles in one corner. 'Pick up those tiles,' she said.

Mary did as she was asked. And underneath the tiles were two bags of gold, a big one and a little one.

The ghost quivered. 'Mary,' she said, 'that big bag is for

your master. But that little bag is for you, for you are a dauntless girl and deserve it.'

Before Mary could open the bag or even open her mouth, the old ghost drifted up the steps and out of sight. She was never seen again and Mary had a devil of a time groping her way along the dark passage and up out of the cellar.

After three days the squire came back from London.

'Good morning, Mary,' he said. 'Have you seen anything of my mother while I've been away?'

'Yes, sir,' said Mary. 'That I have.' She opened her eyes wide. 'And if you aren't afraid of coming down into the cellar with me, I'll show you something.'

The squire laughed. 'I'm not afraid if you're not afraid,' he said, for the dauntless girl was a very pretty girl.

So Mary lit a candle and led the squire down into the cellar, walked along the passage, took a right turn and a left, and raised the loose tiles in the corner for a second time.

'Two bags,' said the squire.

'Two bags of gold,' said Mary. 'The little one is for you and the big one is for me.'

'Lor!' said the squire, and he said nothing else. He did think that his mother might have given him the big bag, as indeed she had, but all the same he took what he could.

After that, Mary always crossed the knives and forks at mealtimes to prevent the old ghost from telling what she had done.

The squire thought things over: the gold and the ghost and Mary's good looks. What with one thing and another he proposed to Mary, and the dauntless girl, she accepted him. In a little while they married, and so the squire did get one hand on the big bag of gold after all.

'What was the song, Davie?'
'Never mind the song – it was the
singing that counted.'

AN OLD MAN IN SUFFOLK

SOURCES & NOTES

Sources and notes for those who would like to search out the originals, or to visit some of the places and sights mentioned in these tales.

Yallery Brown. 'Legends of the Lincolnshire Cars' by Mrs M. C. Balfour in *Folk-Lore*, Volume II, Folk-Lore Society, London, 1891.

Under the general headings of 'Legends of the Cars' and 'Legends of the Lincolnshire Cars' Mabel Balfour – a niece of Robert Louis Stevenson – printed nine astonishing Lincolnshire folk-tales in the journal *Folk-Lore* during 1891. I have included seven of them in this book. In each case, I have kept very close to the original but have modified the heavy Lincolnshire dialect.

This is Yallery Brown's song and why the dialect needs modifying!

> *Wo'k as thou wull*
> *Thou'll niver do well;*
> *Wo'k as thou mowt*
> *Thou'll niver gain owt;*
> *Fur harm an' mischaunce an' Yallery Brown*
> *Thou's let oot thy-sel' fro' unner th' sto'an.*

The Pedlar of Swaffham. *The Diary of Abraham de la Pryme* edited by Charles Jackson, The Surtees Society, 1870. Reprinted by J. Glyde in *The Norfolk Garland*, London, 1872, which has an additional section about how the first treasure found by John Chapman had a Latin inscription on the lid. The earliest account of this story I have found is in Blomefield's *A Topographical History of the County of Norfolk*, 1739–75.

In 1462, a pedlar (or chapman) paid for the new north aisle of Swaffham Church in Norfolk, and contributed to the cost of the spire. This is recorded in the fifteenth-century Black Book which is still in Swaffham Church Library, and which includes a list of benefactors to the church. The rebuilding of the church was actually begun in 1452 but not completed until the middle of the sixteenth century. You can see it today; you can see fragments of John Chapman's chair (carved with the figure of a pedlar with a pack on his back and a mastiff at his side) and of stained glass (which showed the pedlar with his wife and three children); you can see the spire, a pointed reminder, from miles off.

I have added to the original many details to give a picture of the fifteenth-century journey to London.

The Suffolk Miracle. *English and Scottish Popular Ballads*, edited by F. J. Child, Boston, 1857–9. Child reprinted the ballad from a broadside in the Roxburghe Collection.

The rather sketchy ballad does not really do justice to this haunting and widely-known story. Child writes: 'A tale of a dead man coming on horseback to his inconsolable love, and carrying her to his grave, is widely spread among the Slavic people and the Austrian Germans, was well known a century ago among the northern Germans, and has lately been recovered in the Netherlands, Denmark, Iceland and Brittany.'

I have departed from the original in allowing Rosamund to be present when her lover's grave is opened, given names to the protagonists, and generally tried to add a little colour and suspense to the ballad's pace.

What A Donkey! 'The Metamorphosis' in *Facetiae Cantabrigienses*, London, 1825.

The theme of the thief who claims to have been changed into an ass or a donkey is common to the folk-tales of many European countries, including France and Spain, Holland and Germany, Lithuania, Italy and Hungary, and there is also a Philippine version of the story.

Long Tom and the Dead Hand. 'The Dead Hand' in 'Legends of the Lincolnshire Cars' by Mrs M. C. Balfour in *Folk-Lore II*, iii, London, 1891.

In her foreword, Mrs Balfour writes that the Cars of the Ancholme valley 'are still worth seeing, and have a beauty, or rather an attraction of their own. Stunted willows mark the dyke-sides, and in winter there are wide stretches of black glistening peat-lands and damp pastures; here and there great black snags work their way up from submerged forests below. When the mists rise at dusk in shifting wreaths, the bleak wind from the North Sea moans and whistles across the valley, it is not difficult to people the Cars once more with all the uncanny dwellers, whose memory is preserved in the old stories.'

Shonks and the Dragon. *The History of Hertfordshire* by Nathaniel Salmon, London, 1728; *The Folklore of Hertfordshire* by Doris Jones-Baker, London, 1977; *Albion – A Guide to Legendary Britain* by Jennifer Westwood, London, 1985.

The tombstone of Sir Piers Shonks lies in a recess in the north wall of the nave of Brent Pelham Church. And above it is a tablet with the inscription:

> *Nothing of Cadmus nor St. George, those names*
> *Of great renown, survives them but their fames;*
> *Time was so sharp set as to make no Bones*
> *Of theirs, nor of their monumental Stones.*
> *But Shonks one serpent kills, t'other defies,*
> *And in this wall as in a fortress lies.*

These lines, telling us that Shonks first killed a dragon and then out-witted the devil by having himself buried inside a wall (a motif that occurs in several British folk-tales) were probably written in the late sixteenth century. The tombstone, however, dates from the thirteenth century while Piers Shonks may well be one Peter Shank who lived in Brent Pelham in the fourteenth century. So we can say the legend as we know it today, combining two elements (dragon-slaying and tricking the devil), took shape between four and six hundred years ago.

To my ear, Shonks sounds a rather improbable name for a dragon-slayer. So I've introduced a little humour into the story, and am also responsible for giving our hero a daughter and having her attend on Sir Piers when he fights the dragon.

The Devil Take the Hindmost. *Highways and Byways of East Anglia* by William A. Dutt, London, 1904.

Like 'Shonks and the Dragon', this is a story with two elements: the death of a poacher and the appearance of a phantom coach. It is impossible to say when they first became connected.

In her splendid *Everyman's Book of English Folk Tales*, Sybil Marshall says, 'Though the Devil is not specifically mentioned, one is left with the feeling that he certainly had some hand in the mysterious end of George Mace.' I have developed this idea a little in the interests of dovetailing the two parts of the story.

This is one of several Norfolk tales describing the appearance of a phantom coach. Another tells how Anne Boleyn visits Blickling Hall (where she lived as a girl) every year on the night of her execution. Anne rides in a black hearse drawn by four headless horses; she is dressed in white and her own head lies in her lap.

Breckles Hall, once an Elizabethan manor and now a farmhouse, lies three or four miles south-east of Watton, a small town midway between Thetford and East Dereham.

Tom Tit Tot. *Ipswich Journal*, 15, 1878, contributed by Mrs A. Walter Thomas.

Mrs Walter Thomas says she heard this wonderful tale as a young girl from her old west Suffolk nurse. It is the English counterpart to the Grimms' tale of 'Rumpelstilzchen' (*Kinder-und-Hausmärchen*, 1812).

In his *English Fairy Tales*, Joseph Jacobs noted: 'One of the best folk-tales that has ever been collected, far superior to any Continental variants of this tale with which I am acquainted.'

The Gipsy Woman. *East Anglian, VII*, 1897–8, contributed by Miss L. A. Fison and her sister Mrs A. Walter Thomas.

This tale, heard by the contributors from their nurse (see above) is a charming sequel to 'Tom Tit Tot' – and it's worth mentioning that the version of 'Tom Tit Tot' printed in *Merry Suffolk* (1899) ends with the words: 'Lork! How she did clap her hands for joy. "I'll warrant my master'll ha' forgot all about spinning next year," says she.'

The Dead Moon. 'Legends of the Lincolnshire Cars' by Mrs M. C. Balfour in *Folk-Lore, II*. Folk-Lore Society, London, 1891.

Mrs Balfour says that she heard the story from a girl of nine, a cripple, who had heard it from her grandmother. 'But I think,' she writes, 'it was tinged by her own fancy, which seemed to lean to eerie things, and she certainly revelled in the gruesome descriptions, fairly making my flesh creep with her words and gestures.'

The Green Children. *Chronicon Anglicanum* by Ralph of Coggeshall, Rolls Series No. 66 (Rerum Brittanicarum medii aevi scriptores), 1857. Reprinted, Brussels, 1963.

Ralph was Abbot of the Cistercian monastery at Little Coggeshall from 1207–1217 AD, and a lively chronicler of English history. His contemporary, William of Newbridge, also recorded this story in his *Historia Rerum Anglicarum*. He said that the green children were found at Woolpit (named after the Wolf Pits) four or five miles from Bury St Edmunds in Suffolk. He also records that the green girl said that her country was called St Martin's Land, because the saint was worshipped there, and that the people there were Christians.

William of Newbridge set the story in the reign of King Stephen (1135–54) and so have I, in this retelling, and in my libretto for the children's opera composed by Nicola Le Fanu. But the idea of little people coming up out of the earth is far older than that. It is age-old, but each age claims it as its own.

Sea Tongue. 'The Undersea Bells' in *Forgotten Folk-Tales of the English Counties*, by Ruth Tongue, London, 1970.

The tale was collected from Norfolk fishermen in 1905 and 1928 by the Reverend John Tongue, who was at one time Vicar of

Mundesley. The tale of a church bell or bells pealing under the water is common to several places along the Norfolk and Suffolk coast, including Dunwich, as well as to Cardigan Bay and the Lancashire coast.

I see my 'fractured narrative' as a kind of sound-story for different voices (or for one voice taking the different parts). The form of the story relates it to 'The Wildman', the other coastal tale in this collection, and owes something to the idea that everything in our universe, every stick and stone, has its own voice.

The Spectre of Wandlebury. *Otia Imperialia* by Gervase of Tilbury (ca. 1212 AD), edited by F. Liebrecht, Hanover, 1856.

The Iron Age hill-fort known as Wandlebury Camp crowns the Gogmagog Hills near Cambridge. Below it, there was once a hill-carving of a giant called Gogmagog (at one time a generic name for a giant), and maybe also more ancient carvings of long-forgotten gods.

A Pitcher of Brains. 'A Pottle of Brains' in 'Legends of the Cars' by Mrs M. C. Balfour in *Folk-Lore II, ii*. London, 1891.

The Black Dog of Bungay. *The Table Book of Daily Recreation and Information, and Year Book* by W. Hone, London, 1833. Reprinted by E. S. Hartland (editor) in *County Folk-Lore*, Volume I: Suffolk, Folk-Lore Society, London, 1895.

This event, subtitled 'A Strange and Terrible Wunder', is said to have taken place on Sunday 4th August, 1557, at Holy Trinity Church, Bungay, on the border of Norfolk and Suffolk. One version (the one I have followed) tells of two people being killed and one severely burned while attending morning service; another says that two men were 'Sleyn in the Tempest in the Belfry in Time of Prayer'. The dog was seen on the same day at Blibery Church, seven miles from Bungay, where he killed two men and a boy, and burned the hand of another.

I have introduced the idea of two villagers on their way to church, and dramatised a story which reads in the original like a newspaper report.

That's None of Your Business. *Folk-Lore, III,* London, 1892, contributed by Lady Camilla Gurdon.

Lady Gurdon was told this snippet by her gardener and his wife, in south-east Suffolk.

The Strangers' Share. 'Legends of the Lincolnshire Cars' by Mrs M. C. Balfour in *Folk-Lore, II, iii,* London, 1891.

At the heart of this important tale, which preserves many Lincolnshire beliefs and customs, lies a simple green message about respecting and cherishing the land that gives us life. The Strangers or Greencoaties are earth-spirits, just as Tiddy Mun (see below) is plainly the spirit of swamp and car and marsh and fen.

Cape of Rushes. 'Cap o' Rushes' in *Ipswich Journal,* 1877, contributed by Mrs A. Walter Thomas.

Mrs Walter Thomas heard this tale as a child from an old servant, in all likelihood the nurse who told her 'Tom Tit Tot' and 'The Gipsy Woman' (see above). It was originally called 'Cap o' Rushes'. But since it is clear that the teller meant by 'cap' a cloak with a hood, I have changed 'cap' to 'cape'.

This story, with a beginning that reminds one of *King Lear*, has been collected throughout Europe in more than two dozen versions, and belongs to the very large group of tales (there are more than three hundred of them) known as Cinderella stories.

Samuel's Ghost. 'Legends of the Lincolnshire Cars' by Mrs M. C. Balfour in *Folk-Lore II, iv,* London, 1891.

Mrs Balfour heard this funny-gruesome tale from Fanny, a crippled girl aged nine, who had heard it from her 'gran'. Fanny also told Mrs Balfour the story of 'The Dead Moon'.

The word 'worm' (derived from the Anglo Saxon *wyrm*) means dragon.

Tom Hickathrift. *Chap-Books and Folk-Lore Tracts,* No. 1, edited by G. L. Gomme and H. B. Wheatley for the Villon Society, London, 1885. This is a reprint of the chapbook in the Pepys Library at

Magdalene College, Cambridge, which was printed sometime between 1660 and 1690.

It seems likely that the hero of this story, which incorporates so many traditional motifs, actually existed (though it is impossible to say precisely when), and there are various traditions associating him with the Tilney villages near King's Lynn.

In the original, the death of the giant is followed by the episodes with the footballers, the thieves and the tinker. Since the killing of the giant forms the climax of the tale I have, like Joseph Jacobs, rearranged the running order.

The Wildman. *Chronicon Anglicanum* by Ralph of Coggeshall (ca. 1210 AD).

Ralph tell us that during the reign of Henry II (1154–89), fishermen from Orford in Suffolk 'caught a wildman in their nets'. He was completely naked, and covered in hair. He was imprisoned in the newly-built castle, did not recognise the Cross, did not talk despite torture, returned voluntarily into captivity after having eluded three rows of nets, and then disappeared never to be seen again.

The Green Mist. 'Legends of the Lincolnshire Cars' by Mrs M. C. Balfour in *Folk-Lore, II*. Folk-Lore Society, London, 1891.

I have introduced into the story itself some of the folk customs alluded to in the source's preamble. I have also converted some of the reported action into direct action, with the use of dialogue, and have attempted a description of the green mist itself.

The Callow Pit Coffer. *The Norfolk Garland* edited by John Glyde, London, 1872.

Southwood is a little hamlet lying between Norwich and Great Yarmouth. When the Church of St Edmund at Southwood (it was a thatched church) fell into disrepair in 1881, the iron ring from Callow Pit was taken to the neighbouring parish of Limpenhoe and fastened to the church door. It is there now.

I have chosen to set the story in the reign of King Stephen (1135–54) and introduced a supporting cast of villagers.

A Coggeshall Calendar. 'The Coggeshall Jobs' in *A Dictionary of British Folk-Tales* by Katharine M. Briggs, London, 1970–1.

No less than forty-five places in England are traditionally said to be inhabited by noodles or simpletons, including Gotham in Nottinghamshire (subject of the *Merie Tales of the Mad Men of Gotam*, published in the first half of the sixteenth century), Borrowdale in Westmoreland (Cumbria), St. Ives in Cornwall and the whole of the Isle of Wight! They all have light-hearted anecdotes similar to these (in some cases the same as these) told against them.

Tiddy Mun. 'Legends of the Lincolnshire Cars' by Mrs M. C. Balfour, in *Folk-Lore, II*. Folk-Lore Society, London, 1891.

Tiddy Mun is the spirit of the fen country. Mrs Balfour heard the story from an old woman who had lived all her life in the Cars, 'who in her young days herself observed the rite she describes, though she would not confess to it within the hearing of her grandchildren, whose indifference and disbelief shocked her greatly. To her, 'Tiddy Mun' was a perfect reality, and one to be loved as well as feared.'

The Dauntless Girl. *The Recreations of a Norfolk Antiquary* by Walter Rye, Norwich, 1920. Reprinted from the Norton Collection (MS. six volumes).

I have kept close to the original, only stopping to modify the dialect and to put a few words into the mouths of the farmer's drinking companions.

SOURCES OF
SHORT QUOTATIONS

p.1 An old man in Lincolnshire.

p.11 Anonymous and widely printed. Possibly by Sir Walter Raleigh.

p.26 *The Pastons: A Family in the Wars of the Roses* edited by Richard Barber (1981). Letter from Margery Brews to John Paston III.

p.34 *An Hour Glass on the Run* by Alan Jobson (1959). A rhyming notice in a pub on the Broads.

p.38 *Norfolk Fowler* by Alan Savory (1953).

p.48 *Chronicles* by John de Trokelow continued by Henry de Blaneford (1866). The events described are said to have taken place in 1405.

p.57 *I Walked by Night* by George Baldry, edited by Lilias Rider Haggard (1935).

p.64 Traditional (Suffolk shepherds).

p.72 *Lavengro* by George Borrow (1851).

p.77 J. Wentworth Day in *The East Anglian Magazine* (c. 1950).

p.90 *Norfolk Life* by Lilias Rider Haggard (1943).

p.103 Edward Thomas in a letter to Gordon Bottomley (January 15th, 1908).

p.110 'Sweet Suffolk Owl' by Thomas Vautor. Cited in *East Anglian Verse* chosen and edited by E. A. Goodwyn and J. C. Baxter (1974).

p.118 Pal Hall's Quiffs from *A Dictionary of British Folk-Tales* by Katharine M. Briggs (1970–1). Pal Hall was William Peak Hall, a Cambridge builder. He flourished in about 1880.

p.126 *People and Places in Marshland* by Christopher Marlowe (1927).

p.132 Traditional.

p.135 *A Tour through Britain* by Daniel Defoe (1722).

p.143 *The Norfolk Garland* by John Glyde (1872).

p.149 *Town and Country Magazine; or Universal Repository of Knowledge, Instruction and Entertainment* (1770).

p.154 'The Norfolke Turnippe' *An Auncient Tale*, Anonymous.

p.167 *The Shore Shooter* by Alan Savory (1956). First published as *Lazy Rivers*.

p.173 *A Norfolk Garland* by John Glyde (1872).

p.181 *A History of Norfolk* (Popular County Histories) by Walter Rye (1887).

p.192 Collection (MS) by F. J. Norton cited in *A Dictionary of British Folk-Tales* by Katharine M. Briggs (1970–1).

p.197 Verses from a seventeenth-century song ('Powte's Complaint') against the Fen draining schemes, cited in *East Anglia in Verse and Prose* edited by Angus Wilson (1982) (*powte: sea-lamprey*).

p.206 *Chronicon Anglicanum* by Ralph of Coggeshall, fl. 1207–18 (1857). Translated by Kevin Crossley-Holland.

p.215 'Davie' in *Akenfield* by Ronald Blythe (1969).

Acknowledgements

The author and publishers wish to acknowledge their debt in general for the use of the above quotations; in particular for p.26 to Boydell & Brewer for kind permission to use the quotation from *The Pastons: A Family in the Wars of the Roses* by Richard Barber (Woodbridge, 1981); the Haggard Estate for the extract from Lilias Rider Haggard's *Norfolk Life* (1943) on p.90; and for p.118 to Routledge & Kegan Paul for kind permission to use the quotation from *A Dictionary of British Folk-Tales* by Katharine Briggs (London, 1970–71).

GLOSSARY

archery butts
: a mark or target for archery practice. By law every male peasant had to possess a longbow and arrows and practise regularly at the butts.

balk
: a ridge.

boggart, bogle
: both are kinds of bogie, which is the name for a wide range of spirits who mislead human beings. Boggarts are, on the whole, no worse than mischievous while bogles can be frightening and dangerous.

bull's noon
: midnight.

chapman
: a pedlar. People were often called by their professions: for instance, Butcher, Cooper, Taylor, Smith.

the Chronicle
: the Anglo-Saxon Chronicle, a year by year history of England inspired by King Alfred and continued up to 1154, the end of the reign of King Stephen.

clappers
: castanets.

cottar
: a peasant, a cottager who owned an acre or two of his own but had to do a certain amount of work on his lord's land.

demesne
: estate, land.

Edmund — a ninth-century King of the East Anglians and once the patron saint of England. He was killed by the Danes in 869.

flitch — a 'side' of bacon, salted and cured.

the Gold Road — a road from Lynn, the major port in Norfolk, to London. It was so called because of the stream of valuable exports and imports carried along it.

gourd — a drinking bottle made from the hollowed shell of the gourd fruit.

humstrum — a one-stringed roughly-made musical instrument.

Lammas Day — August 1st.

mastiff — a powerful dog with a large head, drooping ears and pendulous lips.

mothering cakes — cakes eaten on Mothering Sunday, which falls on the second last Sunday of Lent.

mugwort, mayweed, crab-apple, thyme, fennel — different herbs, used as medicines.

open fields — the arable land of an ordinary village, cultivated in two great open fields which were divided into strips belonging to the cottars and their lord.

pardoner — a man authorised by the Pope to forgive sins in return for money. Sometimes pardoners were rascals, and thieved from the poor.

portmanteau — a case or bag, usually made of leather, for carrying money, clothing and other necessaries.